A
Gentleman
for
Christmas

Kassian instantly draws you into the past with accurate and incredibly realistic imagery. This love story goes beyond the usual tropes with a clash of cultures and social status that will have you groaning in frustration, even as you root for the charming and lovable characters. A sweet, historical, Christmas treasure you'll read over and over.

— KATIE O'CONNOR

Class and country provide the conflict in this delightful Christmas romance with a poignant message. Add a plumb pudding, festive music, a Scottish hero — and you've got all the ingredients for a wonderful holiday read.

— ROXY BOROUGHS

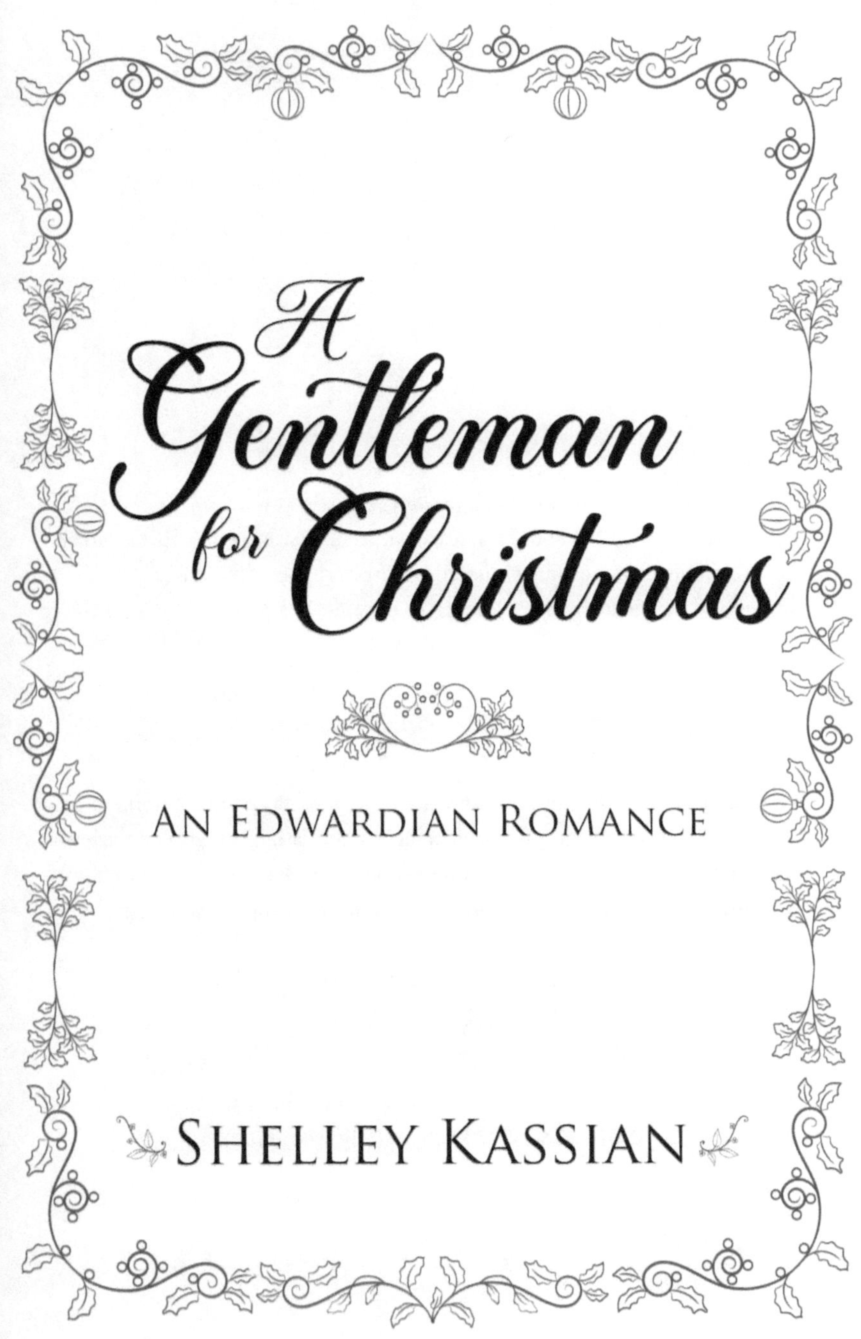

A Gentleman for Christmas

An Edwardian Romance

Shelley Kassian

Published 2021 by Shelley Kassian
(shelleykassian.com)

ISBN: 978-1-7770699-8-8 (Print Edition)
ISBN: 978-1-7770699-9-5 (Digital Edition)

Design and cover art by 100 Covers
Copyediting by Ted Williams

DEDICATION

For my mom, Inez Kelemen
This novel is for you!

ACKNOWLEDGMENTS

This novel was first published in the anthology: *Hugs, Kisses and Mistletoe Wishes*. I wish to thank my colleagues; Roxy Boroughs, S.L. Dickson, Raine Hughes, Ellen Jorgy, Katie O'Connor, Sherile Reilly, and A.M. Westerling for their assistance in creating a sweet collection of Christmas romance stories. Without their vision for a holiday anthology, I honestly don't think *A Gentleman for Christmas* would have been written.

Much thanks to Katie O'Connor, my critique partner, for beta-reading this novel prior to publication.

Thank you to my mom for sharing her memories of her grandparents, which inspired such things as Christmas pudding. The recipe described in this book came from "Modern Cookery for Private Families," authored by Eliza Acton and first published in 1864.

Credit to Ted Williams for copyediting the manuscript.

Much thanks to 100 Covers for my beautiful cover, featuring Logan and Cecily in front of the heroine's home.

And finally, thanks to my amazing readers for supporting me by buying this book! I couldn't do this work without your support.

CHAPTER ONE

NOVEMBER 19, 1905

Stir-it-up Sunday.

Cecily drove the horse-drawn cutter across fields thick with snow, tolerating the change in the weather. The blizzard the day before had blown in a miserable cold, forcing everyone in Essex to seek shelter from the storm. If the temperature hadn't fallen to a bitter thirty below, Cecily would have paralleled the winter scenery to a Victorian Christmas card: grasslands blanketed with snow, weeping spruces thick with frost, and the odd currant bush sequined with crystallized pearls. She flipped the reins, finding beauty in winter.

"Come on, Cisco," she said, urging the horse to run, "give us a good trot, will you."

Abigail squirmed on the bench seat, bundled in a thick fur

coat and heavy woolen blankets. She shifted closer to her. "I'm glad we brought the blankets. The scenery is pretty, but the frost in the air has me chilled to the bone. The weather's not fit for man nor beast."

"What did you expect?" Cecily asked. "It's the third week of November. Winter arrives whether we like it or not. Sunshine and pleasant weather never last."

Abigail pouted. "I'm not sure I expected anything."

"I know you with your visions of sugar plums dancing in your head. You hoped for the impossible, that a warmer than usual fall would never come to an end."

"Sure, it's true, I wasn't ready for this beastly weather. Can you blame me? Who doesn't love the summer months? You're not telling me anything I don't already know."

Cecily tsked her tongue. "I get it...you're unhappy, the farmers are unhappy, no one wants winter to come. Not even me. Everyone's complaining that the snow fell too soon. There's still crops on the fields."

"Father's not happy, and his new racehorse hasn't done anything to brighten his spirits. He's been in a surly mood for days."

"It wasn't the expense that upset him. Poor Papa, he's disappointed racing season is over," Cecily said, making a face. "Winter always arrives, no matter that one might wish it otherwise."

"There's one positive," Abigail said, glancing longingly at a six-foot spruce. "Winter brings us closer to the magic of Christmas."

Cecily pondered Abigail's whimsical expression. The

closer they came to Advent the merrier her disposition. Who could blame her? The season imparted tidings of joy. A time of caroling, families gathering, and presents under the tree. Plenty of reasons to celebrate. "Is that why you're smiling? Or maybe you fancy the Campbell tree?"

Abigail giggled; the wintry cold caused steam to waft from her lips. "It's a fine tree. A full skirt at the bottom and its branches are nicely rounded to the top. I can imagine what it would look like with a silver garland and lit candles adorning the greenery. I wonder…"

Cecily snapped the reins, her eyebrows rising. "Forget it. It's not possible."

"Why not? Logan would give it to us. We only need to ask him."

Cecily blushed, simply from hearing their neighbor's name, but she wondered what Abigail was really thinking about? Her sister knew the procedure for selecting a tree and they were never included in the process. Abigail tried her patience these days, making unusual comments or asking cheeky questions. There was something in her expression that suggested she knew Cecily's deepest held secret.

"Honestly, Abigail, you have a story hidden inside your head of curls, one that's dying to come out. I see it in your eyes. I hear it in your laughter."

Abigail shrugged, smothering a giggle. "You're imagining things. I'm excited about the holidays. Who wouldn't be after the first snowfall? We're traveling to Granny's house to stir up Christmas pudding. I know it's cold outside, but the snow reminds me of my favorite season. Does it not do the same for you? What do you want for Christmas, Cecily?"

What did she want? Logan Campbell came to mind. He'd make a nice gift. Wrapped with a golden tie bow, she'd seek him beneath the mistletoe, hoping for a clandestine kiss, but wanting a gentleman for Christmas seemed inappropriate.

"I haven't had much time to think about it. A new dress or a pair of shoes would suit nicely, though I suspect a pair of socks or mittens might be in the works. I've heard mother's needles clicking at night."

"It's not what I thought you'd say," Abigail said, a whimsical expression on her face.

Cecily glanced at her sister, suspecting an undercurrent of mischief. "Oh, what did you think I'd say? Shoes from Paris? A piece of jewelry? One could only hope."

"It's nothing. Forget it."

But Cecily wasn't imagining her sister's odd behavior. Abigail's persistence caused Cecily to consider gifts that a woman might desire to receive rather than material objects. Her thoughts gave way to Logan Campbell. Again. They'd passed a tree, the spruce belonging to the Campbell family and one handsome son.

He'd caught her attention a few seasons ago when the Campbell family purchased the neighboring land. Given they were of similar age, Logan had attended the same one-room schoolhouse. He had a Scottish heritage and with her customs being English, her father hadn't supported their friendship. In fact, Papa had not spoken kindly of the Scottish family living near his farm, and that opinion hadn't changed when Logan became a veterinary surgeon.

He had a reputation as an animal whisperer. Logan could whisper in her ear any day, even on Sundays, but having a skill with animals didn't matter to Papa. John Carleton was particular about his horses and their care. His ignorance irritated Cecily, and likely had encouraged her feelings to rise to the surface. She'd loved Logan from the start. A woman's heart sang its own songs and she'd found herself dreaming about the Scottish gentleman.

Had she voiced a sentimental word in her sleep? Is this why her sister was pestering her?

"Leave off, Abigail," Cecily said, rounding the corner of the Campbell property. That's when the man of her dreams came toward them, riding a large draft horse. Cecily urged Cisco to a stop.

"Good morning, lassies," Logan said, his breath steaming from his lips.

"Hi, Logan," Cecily said, thinking he'd never looked better. A plaid scarf wrapped around his neck, a Scots bonnet on his head and a gray woolen coat draped across his broad shoulders. A woman could get lost in those hazel eyes. "What brings you out in this miserable weather? It's an unpleasant day to take a ride."

"There's no choice in the matter. A farmer's animal needs care. Are you driving to your grandmother's house?"

Cecily drew in a contemplative breath. "Well, it's time for the yearly stir-it-up. I know the weather's poor, but we promised to help Granny. Mixing the fruit requires arm strength and Granny hurt her hand recently."

"Has she seen a doctor?"

"Not to my knowledge, but Mama assures me the burn isn't serious."

"I know I'm no more than an animal doctor," he said, smiling as if he'd told a joke, "but I'd be happy to check on her if you think it's necessary. Some people don't like a visit from the local doctor."

"Kind of you to offer. I'll let you know," Cecily said. "Is your mother mixing today?"

Logan glanced in the direction of his homestead, then at her. "Nah, not today. My mother's been ill. She's felt poorly for more than a month now."

"We're sorry to hear it," Abigail said, nudging Cecily. "Is there anything you need, anything we can do to help?"

Cecily glanced at her sister, wondering why she'd make such an offer. It wasn't proper.

Logan came closer, his horse meandering to Cecily's side of the sleigh. "She hasn't been able to cook. The smell of food spoils her appetite. My brothers and I, well, we're helpless in the kitchen, yet we've done our best to help. Little sister is too young to go near the range."

"Isla's four?"

"Yes, she's still playing with her dolls," Logan said, staring at her in an appealing way.

Cecily took a deep breath, dreamily staring at his eyes and ginger tendrils of hair that escaped his Scots bonnet. She wanted to help him, but what could she do? Assisting the

Campbells could bring on Papa's wrath, and though her father was a good man, his sternness could be a problem. No one liked him when he was angry.

"We'll keep your family in our thoughts and prayers, and we wish your mother a speedy recovery."

"If you're of a mind to help, maybe we could make a trade. Good trees on this land and lumber's important this time of year. I could cut a few logs for Mr. Carleton. I could help him with his horses."

"We saw a tree that would make the *perfect* trade," Abigail said.

The comment upset Cecily. Why would her sister make such an offer? "Abigail, don't be impertinent."

"Cecily's not a half bad cook either." Abigail winked. Logan's eyebrows rose.

Cecily's face heated, flaming with irritation. A response was long in the coming, though she did kick Abigail's foot. They had servants. She seldom cooked anything. Why was her sister acting out of character?

"I'll speak to Father," Cecily said, glancing at her sister, giving her a warning look. "I hope your mother gets better soon, but we won't keep you. We must be on our way to Granny's house."

"Of course, I have to go as well."

"A good day to you, Logan."

He stroked his hat, giving her a meaningful look. "Nice to see you, Cecily. You too, Abigail."

"And you, Logan." Cecily flipped the reins. "Away we go, Cisco."

After they travelled a short distance and were out of earshot of Logan, Cecily minded her sister. "What was that about?"

Abigail gave her a pleading look. "You have to help him, Cecily, you'll never have a better reason to get closer to Logan."

"What are you talking about?"

Abigail pulled the blanket tighter around her shoulders. "It's obvious, Cecily, at least to me. You like Mr. Campbell."

Why would Abigail say such a thing? Cecily's brain hurt thinking about it. Yes, she liked Logan, but she wasn't ready to disclose this information to anyone. Certainly not her sister. "I do not."

"Yes, you do."

"What gives you that impression?"

Her face wrinkled into a frown. "Well, there was that night when I had a bad dream, and you let me sleep in your bed."

"Yes, what of it?"

Cecily waited patiently for an answer. Abigail glanced at her, nibbling at her bottom lip, trying hard to conceal the truth. "You've always had a talent for talking in your sleep."

Cecily's face heated, despite the cold, her cheeks flushing a rosy hue of pink. "What did you hear?"

"Not much," Abigail said nervously. "A few silly words and Logan's name."

Cecily swallowed, wishing she could escape her embarrassment. "On pain of your life, Abigail, promise me you'll not tell anyone what you think you've heard, not

Mother, not Father. I like Logan, but no matter what the heart yearns for, there are practical matters to consider."

"What could be more practical than love?"

This *feeling* wasn't love. This crush on a handsome neighbor bordered on obsession. Cecily couldn't get him out of her mind. She thought about him constantly. His perfect face, his hazel eyes, his full kissable lips. Talking in her sleep? How could she keep this fixation with Logan to herself?

"Whoa, sister. I don't have feelings for Logan. We're not even close friends." He was only a sweet flirtation in her dreams, a secret crush, and could never be more than that.

Abigail's eyebrows rose as if questioning her sincerity. "You could love him."

She certainly wanted a relationship with Logan Campbell. What lady wouldn't? She'd heard the gossip from the neighbors. Gentle care administered to animals. Respect accorded to people in the community. No matter what anyone said, a relationship with Logan Campbell wasn't possible. "Father would never permit it."

"This isn't England. These fields are coated with milk and honey."

"These fields are snowed in with hardship and bitter cold." Cecily laughed, nudging her sister's arm. "Dear sister, I don't see it the same way. We may have begun a new life in a new country, but the cultural differences created in our homeland traveled with us across the sea. They separate us, even though Logan and I are neighbors. I would like to help the Campbells, though Father won't trade anything with a Scot, and that includes his daughter."

"Cecily, you couldn't be more wrong. Our father is a giving man, especially when he knows a family is struggling. He'll help the Campbell family. I know he will."

"Maybe when he loses his hard head," Cecily said, sighing. "Let me think about it."

Though there wasn't much to consider. Cecily knew her father was strong-willed, and talking about probable scenarios seemed pointless. A man's opinion wasn't easily changed. It was best to alter the direction of their conversation.

"Let's focus on getting to Granny's house and stirring up a dessert that will remind us of your favorite time of year. Christmas pudding… It requires a bit of arm muscle and a lot of patience. Do you think you have the strength to stir?"

"I'm more than equal to the work." Abigail gave her a determined look. "I'll help you stir the pot. A dessert suitable for our family and one certain gentleman."

CHAPTER TWO

Logan watched the sleigh as it passed out of sight, his thoughts on Cecily Carleton. He'd fallen for her the first time he'd heard her sing in the church choir, but he was hesitant to confess his feelings. What if she turned him down, breaking his heart?

He wanted to court her, and he'd ask John Carleton for permission if he was a braver man, but he'd be holding his heart in his hands, a heart that could be squashed. It was well and good to frequent the same church service with farmers who toiled over similar lands, facing similar struggles, but to court an Englishman's daughter? Could it be possible?

Logan imagined Mr. Carleton wouldn't even permit him to take care of his prized horses, even though Logan was a trained veterinary surgeon who knew a thing or two about caring for farm animals.

His parents wanted him to court a bonny lassie. A woman who had the same family traditions. Though this new land had more English girls than Scottish. Even so, native lands and family traditions didn't matter much to him. Each Sunday when he looked at Cecily's pretty face, her deep brown hair escaping her bonnet, her angelic voice causing the congregation to stare at her wistfully, well…he only had eyes for her and wouldn't mind building new traditions.

This land wasn't Scotland. It wasn't England either. The Canadian frontier where his family had purchased three acres of farmland delivered long cold winters. A man needed a pillow to lay his head. A wife like Cecily to keep him warm when the nights were cold.

He slapped the reins and urged his draft horse into a trot, his thoughts returning to a local farmer's sickly animal.

CHAPTER THREE

Cecily drove the sleigh toward her grandparents' property. She could barely discern the land from the laneway with all the snow. Ribbons of white unfurled toward the lilac trees and caragana shrubbery that grew near the house. The Queen Anne home gave off pleasant memories even though their family hadn't lived in this country for more than a decade. Yet on foul days such as this, days when a person worried about their skin freezing, days when one was better off to stay inside, Cecily wished her family still lived in Ironbridge, facing rain instead of snow.

In front of the house, Cecily reined-in Cisco, urging the horse to stop, then shifted the brake into place. Her grandfather came round the building and greeted them. "Hi, Grandpa," Cecily said, exiting the sleigh.

"Hi, girls," he replied, grasping Cisco's halter. The horse tossed its head as if it was happy to arrive, or perhaps to say hello. "How was the journey?"

"It's a beast of a day. A strong wind as we passed across the Campbells' land, but we made it through in good time. You have a twinkle in your eye, Grandpa. Is it the frost in the air or are you happy to see us?" Cecily asked, giggling. "Or maybe Cisco earns your smile and your happier to see the horse."

Dressed for the weather, wearing a hat that covered his ears, her grandfather patted Cisco's neck. "He's a beautiful animal, but the shine comes from the cold nipping at my *old* watery eye. But never mind that, I'll care for this handsome fellow. Give him a few oats. He's done well bringing you safely. But you best get inside, your grandmother's been waiting."

"Granny's sharing a family tradition with us today," Abigail said, exiting the sleigh as well. "I can't wait."

"She'll be glad of the help. I'll be glad to sample the pudding on Christmas day, so mind the instructions. Off you go, girls, get inside."

Cecily removed her gloves and strode toward the front entrance, a fur coat and a long woolen dress trailing in the snow. Abigail followed behind her. They were soon climbing the stairs of a wraparound porch. Cecily grasped the doorknob and opened the door. Both sisters passed through the doorway, stomping snow from their shoes in the vestibule. They removed their winter gear and hung the garments on a coat rack, slipped on a pair of indoor shoes and then passed through the breezeway door.

"Hi, Granny, we're here," Abigail called, hurrying toward the kitchen.

Cecily moved at a more leisurely pace, strolling along the hallway, loving the ambience of this character home. A gramophone sat in a corner space. A fire burned in the hearth, giving the room a warm and comfortable atmosphere. This house differed from her grandparents' cottage in England. New memories were fashioning this dwelling into a home. She passed the drawing room and the dining area, lingering, her finger on the doorjamb, dreaming of a day when she might have a place to build her own memories.

Logan Campbell came to mind; ginger hair, hazel eyes, broad shoulders and strong arms that could embrace her, but she suppressed these thoughts. After all, Granny was waiting at the back of the house in the kitchen.

"Hi, girls," Granny called out joyfully, her apron tied around her waist. "My dears, thank you for coming, especially on a chilly day."

The wood stove was lit. Logs burning in the fire box lent warmth to the room. Cecily breathed the aroma of woodsmoke while listening to the odd spark. "The cold can't compete with the Carletons. We're strong souls, made of strong stuff, but where else would we be on stir-it-up Sunday, but with our grandmother," Cecily said, giving her a hug. "Mom told me you needed a helping hand." Granny glanced at her hand momentarily, then gave Cecily a dismissive look.

"Your mother." Granny shook her head, sighing. "The older I get the more she worries."

"Mom said you hurt your hand, and stirring the fruit is not an easy job."

"That cooker." Granny stared at the wood stove as if it

were the enemy. "I'm forever burning my hands, but they'll heal."

"Mama said she offered to send Alice, but you refused."

"I'm fine doing the cooking myself. Did you see your grandfather in the yard?"

Cecily saw the bandage on Granny's right hand, but she didn't comment on the injury. "He's minding Cisco. The poor horse had a difficult run through the snow. He'll need a rest before we can journey home."

"Grandfather will give him a good rubdown, maybe a few oats, too. Shall I put the kettle on? Make us a spot of tea?"

Cecily reached for the kettle. "I'd welcome a hot drink." She filled the kettle from a standing barrel at the back entrance and then returned it to the cooktop and left it there to boil. "It was a cold journey across the fields. Get your apron, Abigail," Cecily said, seeing a stoneware bowl on the worktable. "Shall we roll up our sleeves and get to work?"

"Girls, will you fetch the preserves from the pantry?"

Cecily and Abigail retrieved several crocks.

Once the tea was made, three women went about their work, each of them taking a position at the worktable. Abigail grated dried bread while Cecily measured an equal amount of flour into the bowl.

"Did you happen by any neighbors during your ride?"

Abigail was about to speak, but Cecily shushed her sister, giving her a warning look that silenced her. Granny didn't miss a beat.

"You did see someone. Does this person have a name?"

"Can't put anything past you. By chance, we came across Logan Campbell."

"I wonder why he was out on such a blustery day."

"His mother was ill," Abigail said.

When Cecily elbowed her sister in the ribs, she pouted. "Actually, a farmer required his veterinary services. He mentioned something about a sickly animal. How much fruit do you use in the recipe?"

"Two pounds each of raisins and currants."

"Seems like a lot," Cecily said, measuring the ingredients and then placing them in the bowl.

"Enough for three small puddings."

"Mrs. Campbell is abed," Abigail said, glancing at Cecily warily. "Logan says his mother is unwell."

Granny glanced at Cecily. "You didn't say you talked to him, and I didn't know you were on a first name basis."

"We were crossing his land when we met. Not stopping would have been rude." Cecily's face warmed. Her grandmother's eyes drew together. "What's the next ingredient, Granny?"

"Candied peel," she said quietly, grasping a crock and passing it to Cecily. While she measured the peel, her grandmother placed rinds of one lemon inside the bowl.

"Abigail, will you get the sugar from the pantry?" Granny asked, staring at Cecily. Abigail set off to do the task, pouting, aware that she was being excluded from the conversation.

"How did Mr. Campbell look to you?"

"How did he look?" Cecily asked, her brow furrowing with confusion. Though the question seemed a strange one to ask, Cecily recalled the brief visit. Logan had seemed like a welcome respite from the cold, but she wouldn't confess that being in his company, even temporarily, had been the best part of her day.

"What do you imply? It was cold outside," she said, shaking her head. "He was bundled for the weather; his cheeks were as rosy as Saint Nick's. He was probably dying for us to be on our way so he could get on with his business."

"That's not what I meant. How do you feel about Mr. Campbell?"

"Why do you ask? He's our neighbor. A friend. We went to school together."

Granny's eyebrows drew together. "I have a feeling there's something you're not telling me, and if it's what I suspect, a father doesn't need a reason to disapprove."

The comment frustrated Cecily, so she didn't respond to it. Abigail returned to the worktable, holding a stoneware jar. An awkward silence lingered in the room, and Cecily saw that her sister understood the direction this conversation could go, and gratefully, she kept silent.

"I'm not sure what you're referring to, but I understand the suggestion. Let me speak plainly; Logan Campbell and I don't have a relationship, not much of a friendship either, but if there was something between us, what would be wrong with it? He's a good man. A hardworking man, no different than Papa or Grandpa."

"How much sugar should I put in the bowl?" Abigail asked, appearing worried.

"Two cups," Granny said. Then she stared at Cecily in a

pointed way as Abigail reached for a measuring cup. "He's from a different class of people, and…he's Scottish."

How should she respond to such a comment? Cecily watched her grandmother pinching spices into the bowl: nutmeg, mace, and a tiny bit of salt. She began to speak, then paused. Her grandmother's expression rattled her nerves, indicating she'd revealed too much of her private life. Granny had a knowing look while fetching a bottle of brandy from the cupboard.

Strangely, Abigail came to her defense while pouring sugar into the bowl. "I like Logan. He helped me with my calculations at school. I'm not gifted in mathematics."

"My darling granddaughter, for us women, mathematics only matters in the kitchen. Two cups of brandy are added to this mixture, and at minimum, one dozen eggs."

"Granny, even if I did fancy Logan Campbell, you don't have to worry. He never helped me with my figures, nor does he fancy me."

Granny's expression was not only firm, but also kind. She gave them a sympathetic look, her skin softened with wrinkles from the passing of time, brightening into a curious expression. "I'm not so sure about that. The gentleman didn't let you pass by without seeking conversation." Granny paused as if searching for the right words. "You're beautiful, Cecily. Any man would wish for your hand, but if you were to have a relationship with him, you should know it could create problems for you."

"Granny…"

"Listen to me, Cecily. I'm certain you do like Logan."

Abigail grasped a wooden spoon. "She does, Granny, she dreams of him at night."

"Abigail!" Cecily exclaimed, wanting to whack her sister's backside with the spoon. What was up with her? Her behavior tested Cecily's patience. It was everything she could do to mind her words, but why should she keep her desires hidden?

"Fine, I admit it. I've always liked Logan," Cecily said wistfully, snatching Abigail's spoon. "We went to school together. He's our neighbor." She tore into the pudding and stirred it vigorously. "I can't explain why I value his friendship."

Granny raised her eyebrows while pouring brandy into a cup, then dumped the spirits into the mix. "I can explain it. It's the reality of math. One plus one equals two. Every sheep and ram understands the formula; even so, a Scottish neighbor is well and good until the son comes courting an Englishman's daughter."

"Why are we discussing this? There's no relationship. He hasn't asked Papa for the right to court me, or even asked me to attend a church social."

Cecily kept stirring while Granny poured a second cup of brandy into the mix. "What do you think about this situation, Abigail?"

Abigail took a turn stirring up the fruit mixture. "I wouldn't object. As I said, I like Logan. Father might not welcome a Scottish man into the family, but we're not in England. We should be more welcoming. We come together in the schoolroom and at church. Why can't we come together in friendship outside of these places?"

"And you say Mrs. Campbell is ill?" Granny asked.

"Yes."

"She's likely not cooking much. You could call on the poor woman."

"After the lecture, what are you suggesting?" Cecily asked. "I don't cook."

"I'm suggesting you find out if Mr. Campbell shares your feelings."

"What about Papa…"

"Fathers should never stand in the way of a good ram." Granny gave Cecily a half-smile then fetched three shot glasses and poured an ounce into each, then passed the spirits into their hands. "Fight for what you want. To your future, Cecily."

She stared at the brandy in the shot glass, wondering if sipping the brandy acknowledged her secret desires.

"To Christmas," Abigail toasted them.

The thought of a season filled with comfort and joy made the difference. Cecily clinked her glass with Granny and then her sister, soon swallowing the elixir's heat, but for the life of her, she didn't know if the toast suggested pursuit of something that should have been hidden in her heart.

Abigail smiled at her, still stirring, and she wondered what motivated her sister to pursue the subject in the first place. The only reason she could think of was sweet Abigail wanted something more than a Christmas gift.

"What's next, Granny?"

"Patience." Granny retrieved three damp linen cloths. She stretched them flat on the tabletop. "The secret to binding anything together is ingenuity and patience. Put a generous amount of flour on each tea towel, Cecily."

"Are we talking about cookery, or relationships?"

"Both."

Cecily and Abigail watched their grandmother as she smoothed the flour on the surface of each tea towel. "Now Abigail, you can help by placing an equal amount of fruit mixture on each towel."

Abigail did as Granny asked.

"A family works best when they work together. Abigail, you should not discuss your sister's intentions with anyone. Is that understood?"

"I understand."

Their grandmother's hand seemed sore, yet she tied all three bags and placed them in a large pot to steam.

"Thank you for your help, girls. Obstacles can be overcome, but only if we work together."

"What are the obstacles?" Abigail asked.

Granny laughed, her cheeks coloring to a rosy hue of pink as she said, "Men."

CHAPTER FOUR

After the conversation with Granny, rather than avoiding the notion of a relationship with Logan, Cecily only thought about him more. One morning after she'd broken her fast, she retrieved an easygoing mare and went for a ride, her direction the Campbell farm. Fancy Foot's nostrils flared as they came closer to the green spruce she and Abigail had passed by the previous day.

Cecily paused, supposing the tree would make the perfect Christmas tree, then continued on her way. She'd hoped to see Logan, wishing he'd greet her like he had the day before. She urged the mare to the place they'd met, glimpsing hoof-prints in the snow. But Logan didn't come riding and she wasn't brave enough to venture toward the farmhouse, so she turned the horse around and headed back toward home.

The next time she traveled this way, she'd bring a reason to visit.

CHAPTER FIVE

The first Sunday of Advent embraced the theme of hope. The choir sang a carol they'd been practicing for weeks: *O come, all ye faithful.*

Music had inspired Cecily from the time she was a young girl. This was possibly the reason her mother had encouraged her to join the choir the previous year. The opportunity to sing melodies with like-minded individuals, voices coming together in sweet harmony, gave her and others joy.

Though Cecily had another reason for singing in the choir. Logan attended every service. Though she stood in front of an entire congregation, sharing her gift, she always sang to him.

She wished her father could hear her singing voice, but he refused to attend the service. In fact, he'd never heard her sing with the choir. He wasn't the type of man to be lectured by a minister, about religion or anything else, so only her mother and Abigail watched her performances. Mother would smile when she sang, and she supposed sharing her talent with others was as good a reason as any to be a member of the choir.

Though her family had left the church soon after the service, forcing her to travel home by herself. In the church entranceway, Cecily was putting her picture hat on and fastening the buttons on her coat when she noticed Logan, awkwardly managing his Scots bonnet in his hands.

Was he waiting for her?

"Hi, Logan, are you visiting with someone? I thought you'd left."

He took a sidelong glance, then approached her. "Aye. I was talking to a few of the local lads. Farmers have questions about their livestock and I'm happy to give them advice. Before I knew it, the time got away from me. The choir began singing and I got caught up, listening to the music."

"You stayed to hear the practice?"

He grinned, spinning his hat. "I often can't focus on the minister's sermon." He leaned closer to her in a conspiratorial kind of way. "Don't give up my secret, but it's the choir, not the minister, who inspire me most Sundays."

"The pastor's voice does have a distinctive drone," Cecily whispered, "but there's days I can't match the sopranos' voices, or the hymn falls flat. Margaret only has one good ear and her singing voice booms, joyously, but too loud."

Logan grinned, laughing, his eyes bright. "Your secret is safe with me. I won't tell her what you said. I wouldn't mind if the choral director gave you more solo opportunities. You sound like an angel."

The comment caught her off guard. Logan smiled slightly,

a serene look in his eyes that caused her heart to flutter. Cecily slipped on her gloves, glancing at the floor. "That's kind of you to say, but they'd call me a showboat if I had solo opportunities at every service." If he noticed her discomfort, he didn't draw attention to it.

"Cecily, I saw your mother and sister leaving earlier. It's cold outside. Do you need a ride home? I'd be happy to escort you."

It was a presumptuous thought, yet Cecily wondered if Logan had been waiting for her. Some members of the congregation visited after the service, but most had left by the time the choir finished their practice. She knew she should say no. Logan escorting her home, unchaperoned, it was improper for a lady, but suddenly she didn't care about decorum. Everything in her wanted to say yes.

"I'd be grateful for a ride. Shall we leave?"

Logan extended his arm and she glanced at his hand briefly, but it seemed natural to grasp the crook of his elbow. He felt solid and strong. She glanced at his inquisitive eyes before he escorted her through the doorway and into the breath of winter. He led her across frozen ground toward his cutter. She shielded her face from a gust of wind as they walked across the churchyard. Logan soon assisted her to rise to the bench seat, then gave her a blanket to cover her legs. Then climbing into the sleigh, he urged his draft horse to trot. They were soon thereafter dashing through the snow.

Cecily was quiet for a time while listening to the blades gliding through snow and ice. She studied Logan's gloved hands holding tight to the reins. So much strength in his nimble fingers.

"How's your mother?" Cecily asked. "Has she overcome her illness?"

"Sadly, no. Though the doc has been to the house to see her, I'm beginning to think her condition might not be an illness at all, though my mother hasn't acknowledged the diagnosis."

"I wonder what's making her sick?"

He shook his head. "I don't know."

"But you have an idea."

"I fear I do," Logan said, staring at her in a concerned manner. "Though I didn't wait to drive you home to talk about my mother. Cecily, I need to ask you a question before I lose my nerve."

So, Logan had wanted more than a song or listening to choral music. He'd wanted one of the choir members in his sleigh. A clever man. He knew what he wanted. What did Cecily want? She swallowed as her heart went Pitter Patter.

"It must be important. You seem serious."

He took a deep breath. "It's a serious subject for a man and a woman." Logan pulled on the reins and urged his horse to stop.

"It must be."

Logan didn't look at her while staring at fields of snow. Drawn to his face, she studied his features, strong angular lines, red whiskers on his cheeks. "Life in this country is harsh and often lonely. I'm going to say this before I lose my nerve." He looked at her intently. "Cecily, is there a chance we could be more than neighbors, more than friends?"

Cecily opened her mouth to speak, then didn't say anything. What should she say? *I thought you'd never ask? I've been waiting my entire life for a moment such as this?* He'd placed her in a difficult position. After all her pining for him, the bold approach made her ill-equipped for a proper answer.

Logan flipped the reins. "I've shocked you."

"You've surprised me." Father pressed into her thoughts and Cecily wondered how *he* might respond to the question. Her expression soured.

The draft horse took a step, causing the sleigh to shift slightly. Logan frowned, pulling on the reins. "Well damn, you don't have to say anything. That look in your eyes, the surprise on your face, says all."

Cecily squirmed on her seat, suddenly uncomfortable. What now? One answer was certain. She couldn't live her life based on her father's assertions. "You judge the situation incorrectly. Logan, are you asking to court me?" She raised her gaze to meet his.

He grasped her gloved hand and stared at her in a serious manner. "We're friends, but I have a feeling we could be more. I've had a sense about you. Unless I'm mistaken. Maybe I've been reading that look in your eyes the wrong way."

"How would your mother feel about her son courting an English girl instead of a Scottish lass?" Cecily asked, evading the subject.

"What does our heritage have to do with my mother? It's my business who I see. I'm the oldest in the family, but it's my guess she'd be glad to have one less mouth to feed."

"I wish I could give you an answer, but I'm not at liberty to broach the subject of courtship. I'm a woman, not a man. There are practical matters to consider."

"Like your father and his wealth?"

Cecily frowned. "He wouldn't approve. Regardless that we find ourselves living in a new country, the old people won't let go of their age-old ideals or old ways. You and I, we come from two distinct social classes, never mind the two cultures."

"Who cares about England or Scotland. Cecily, if we lived in a world where you and I were but a man and a woman who found each other's company desirable, if I asked you if you'd court me, how would you reply?"

"I'd say a world where women have the power to make their own decisions doesn't exist. Not yet."

"Please, Cecily. I need to know where I stand."

He stroked her thumb, and his touch surprised her. Cecily welcomed the contact, and though she didn't want to cause conflict in her family, she spoke from the heart.

"I'd say yes."

"You'd say yes." He grinned. "You'd court a guy like me, Logan Campbell."

She clutched his hand. "I don't know what trouble I'm getting myself into by confessing the truth, but…"

"But what?"

"I would welcome a closer friendship."

"You say that as if you're only willing to go so far."

Cecily stared beyond the sleigh at fields of snow that seemed to stretch on forever. The horse neighed, shifted the sleigh a second time, impatient to head toward home. She wasn't eager to do the same. Why hadn't she lied? This truth could cause difficulty in her life, and she didn't want to hurt Logan. "This isn't the English countryside, nor is it Scotland. If we were in our homeland, I'd suggest we run to Gretna Green if your actions were gentlemanly."

"Lassie, we're talking about getting to know each other and forming a closer relationship, not meeting at the altar of marriage just yet."

Cecily shook her head. "Courtship is a serious business. One doesn't begin a relationship without the consideration of marriage. I must be blunt. My father won't welcome whatever is happening between us."

"We're getting ahead of ourselves."

"Are we? What do I do when my father finds out?"

He squeezed her hand in a show of support. "A relationship starts with the couple. It's an optimistic journey, two people believing in each other. A relationship brings hope, no different than the candle that was lit in church this morning. Our parents, in time, might support us."

"Father doesn't hold to religious beliefs. He doesn't attend church. You misunderstand, Logan. I have not said I would court you, only that I'd consider it."

He released her hand, visibly upset. He grasped the reins and encouraged the horse to trot. Away they flew, dashing across fields of snow. The temperature fell. The wind nipped at her face and sorrow filled her soul. Why had she been so vocal?

"I should get you home. I'm suddenly feeling chilled."

"It's not me," Cecily said, sighing. "It's the world we live in. If we decide to have a relationship, we must accept the pathway to friendship, never mind the altar. Logan, this journey could be rocky for both of us."

"I can accept the difficulties. I'm willing to put in the effort."

"Are you? Are you willing to challenge my father's beliefs?"

"Aye, I am. I'm an honest man. I've never been afraid to work for what matters. I'd try to help your father understand. I'd do anything for you, Cecily."

"I don't know if I can give the same effort." Though Cecily wanted to exert the same effort. After all, she'd dreamed of doing so.

Logan didn't respond. Cecily supposed…what could either of them say that might resolve the issue. It wasn't their culture or class status standing in the way of a relationship, their families were the problem.

When they reached Carleton House, Logan stopped the sleigh in the laneway. Cecily didn't want her family to see who had driven her home for fear of repercussions. "Thank you for the ride, Logan."

"A woman like you, I'd take you anywhere."

"Hold on to that thought," Cecily said, exiting the sleigh. "I'm not saying no, but I do need to consider the future."

He gave her a firm stare. "I'll wait, Cecily."

She stood on a frozen patch of ground, watching Logan drive away, wishing she was still sitting beside him. The space stretched between them as he drove into the distance, leaving her bereft and lonely.

She trudged through the snow toward the manor house, her skirts trailing on the ground. A curtain shifted in an upper window and Cecily knew someone had seen the Campbell sleigh. She hoped it was Abigail and not her father.

CHAPTER SIX

Cecily discovered the identity of the person behind the draperies. Her sister.

"I was surprised to see you with Logan," Abigail said while preparing for bed that evening. She stared at Cecily in a curious, tell-me-your-secrets kind of way.

Lying on her bed, Cecily tried to focus on the novel: *The House of Mirth*. She paused in her reading and placed the book on her lap. She glanced at her sister, observing a not-so-innocent young woman drawing a pearl-handled brush through unruly hair. Inquisitiveness brightened her eyes; intrigue creased her lips into a half-smile.

"It's not like you to spy on me."

"It's not like that at all," Abigail replied. "Mother and I should have waited for you. I told her it was too cold for you to walk. Sure, the weather has improved a bit; even so, it's unseasonably cold. The sun goes down earlier in the winter, and…"

"Quit making excuses. You saw us together."

"Yes, I saw you." Abigail confessed. "But Cecily, I was worried." Abigail placed her brush on the vanity and began braiding her unruly hair. A hint of a smile teased her lips upward.

"I'm grateful for your care, dear sister, yet I suspect you have further questions. You have a curious nature." There was no stopping her sister when she had questions.

Abigail glanced at her, smiling. "And is that a terrible trait? Who else can you trust to give advice?" She pivoted on her chair. "Well...will you tell me about him? What was it like, being in his company? What did you talk about? I've been speculating on the reason for the ride all afternoon. Whatever you say, I won't share your confidence with anyone." Abigail touched her lips as if to make a point. "Not even our parents."

Cecily placed her book on the side table, giving Abigail a slight smile. "There's not much to tell. Logan offered to escort me home after choir practice, and as you know, there was a chill in the air."

"There's no better way to warm a woman's heart."

"Did you plan this?" Cecily asked, giggling. "Who could say no to a gentleman on a cold day? I had to accept his offer." And if she were completely honest, with herself, with her sister, she'd accompany Logan in good or bad weather.

"That's not telling me much. What happened?"

"Aren't you a curious little bird. It's sad that the only person I can share this with is my sister. I'd like to sing my news to everyone who would listen. It's frustrating that I must be silent."

"I knew it. Something did happen."

"Little does it matter."

Abigail moved to the bed. "You're dodging my questions; not telling me anything. Cecily, you always go quiet when you want to share but don't think you can. You can trust me. I'm your sister."

Cecily stared at Abigail, at the interest in her eyes. Could she trust her sister? She supposed she should have faith in someone. "All right, Logan asked if he could court me."

Abigail gasped; her eyes brightened. She pressed closer. "He did what? How did you respond?"

"I said no."

Abigail stared at her as if she'd participated in a crime, but now that Cecily considered her courtship response, why had she said no when everything in her had desired to say yes?

"Why would you outright refuse?" Abigail asked, admonishing her like a champion crusader. "He's the knight haunting your dreams. The man you're meant to be with. I don't understand, especially given our recent conversation."

Cecily had made the decision based on her personal beliefs, but as she listened to her sister's entreaty, she questioned not only her decision, but also where Abigail's concern came from. She might be on her side, but she was too passionate. Why did Cecily's relationship with Logan matter to Abigail?

Cecily sighed, tiring of this inquisition. "It wasn't like that. We talked about the obstacles standing in our way."

"Money?" Abigail asked.

"Actually, no. I haven't considered the financial issues."

"Class?"

"There is the consideration that we come from two different social structures, but my concern has more to do with…"

"…Papa." Abigail's breath fizzled out of her like air escaping from a balloon.

"Yes, our dear father. He'll likely not support his daughter if she's courting a Scottish gentleman."

Abigail sighed, then laid on the bed beside her. "Must he linger in the old world? If he's as strict with his children as he is with his stallions and brood mares, he'll likely never accept anything less than perfect for his daughters."

"You're comparing my situation to racehorses?" Cecily asked, her vocal tone expressing surprise.

"Though you cannot appreciate the two concepts—what happens in the stable and the house—I know they connect to each other. It's not fair, Cecily. Father barely knows us, hardly spends time with us. Honestly, why should he care who we see?"

Cecily didn't miss the obvious. Abigail was upset for another reason that was more specific to her situation. "Abigail, the man's our father. I'm certain he only wants the best for us. But why are you apprehensive? Whoever I see doesn't concern you."

"Doesn't it?" Abigail asked, anxiety marring her pretty face.

"What do you mean by that?"

"Let me speak plainly; if you like Logan, and you have the courage to seek your heart's desire, you're forging a new pathway that your sister might follow." Her eyes held a compelling, almost pleading look.

"Ah, I see. So maybe I'm not the only one having dreams at night."

Abigail lowered her eyes and twirled the end of her braid around her finger, wearing a dreamy expression on her face. "Maybe, but I don't talk in my sleep."

"Abigail Carleton, you've been keeping a secret from me."

"Ian Murphy," she said sweetly, disclosing his name, the secret slipping from her lips.

Cecily was surprised she'd acknowledged the truth. "He's Irish."

Abigail didn't refute the comment. "He has the most beautiful eyes I've ever seen."

"Is that so?" Cecily shook her head, giggling at the dreamy tone in her sister's voice.

Abigail twisted on the bed and grasped Cecily's hand. "We can't let our parents dictate our future. The men we court, or who we should fall in love with and marry. Cecily, my heart doesn't work that way. We're both of an age to marry. We can't let Papa or Mama select our husbands. They'll place us in a stuffy manor house."

The vision of an old man came to mind. Cecily thought about Abigail's comment and knew it was true enough. "I don't know what we can do about it."

"I don't know either, but you're older than me. If Papa accepts Logan, maybe he'll accept Ian as well."

"You're scheming," Cecily said, touching her sister's nose. "You'll be fighting for the vote next."

"I'm constantly thinking about how we might change the world. Yet I don't know where to start, but with my sister."

"I'd have to deceive Papa to court Logan. Such a step makes me uncomfortable. I don't know where I'd start."

"The choir," Abigail said, staring at her in a hopeful way.

"What do you mean?"

"Doesn't the choir sing at different congregants' homes every Christmas season? Especially for those in need?"

"Yes, of course, we've been practicing for weeks. Our carols are almost ready."

"Mrs. Campbell has been unwell. If you suggested to Ruth that the choir visit the Campbell family, you'd have a chance to see Logan again, to visit him at his family home."

Cecily liked the idea, liked it very much. "And what would I do, state my claim? Clutch him close to my heart. Hold his hand; say *yes* to courting him?"

"It's taking a risk," Abigail said, nodding, "but if you don't take a chance on what you want, on what will make you happy, you're robbing your own heart of happiness. Will you do what's right for you?"

Cecily contemplated supporting her future and her sister's. "You've given me a lot to think about."

She pondered the idea of approaching the choral director during their mid-week practice, while considering the plusses and minuses of the choir visiting the Campbell farm. In the end, Cecily decided there was only one option. To utilize her vocal cords to their best advantage.

"Silent night, holy night…"

Cecily recommended visiting Mrs. Campbell to the choral director, just like her sister had suggested, and so the evening came to pass. On a night when the sky sparkled with starlight and winter's chill lay heavy in the air, the choir rode on an open sleigh to the Campbells' farm.

When the choral director knocked on the door, Cecily and the other singers were clustered in a semicircle, ready to sing, their choral folders held in their gloved hands. A stern-looking man opened the door, and he indicated with hand gestures that they should leave. This action didn't prevent the singers from offering comfort and joy. They began singing:

"Silent night—holy night—"

He raised his hand a second time, frustration wrinkling his face, but his temperament changed when a frail woman joined him in the entranceway. Shortly thereafter, a family of at least ten people stood in the entryway of the home, listening to the carolers. Cecily held her leather-bound folder, singing, but all the while she watched for the real objective behind this visit.

Logan Campbell.

He appeared in the doorway and stepped out into the night. Tall and well-built, ginger hair and full kissable lips, he wore a lambswool sweater to protect him from the cold. His breath steamed from his lips while Cecily sang: "All is bright…"

She glanced at him occasionally while performing, singing *O Come, All Ye Faithful,* which set off contemplative expressions on the family's faces. Children of varying ages clapped their hands. A young girl with ginger ringlets peered between Mr. Campbell's legs. But when Cecily sang the first verse of the carol, *O Holy Night*, Logan's mother's eyes glistened with unshed tears. Music had a way of reaching pain and discomfort in ways practical acts of kindness could never reach. Cecily saddened to see Mrs. Campbell cry.

The rest of the choir joined in the singing. Cecily knew Logan was watching her the entire time. A chill lingered in the air, but the shiver that tickled her spine had more to do with Logan's heady perusal than the cold. When the singing finished, the Campbell family clapped.

"Thank you," Mrs. Campbell said, wiping her eyes. "I won't forget this visit. Won't you come inside and have some tea? The air is full of frost tonight."

"We'd love to, but you've been ill, and we don't want to burden you," Ruth, the music director said. "We're here to sing, to add joy during the Christmas season. Not to create further work."

Mrs. Campbell didn't say much in response. She glanced at her husband in appeal. He frowned, but then clutched her hand, perhaps offering his support. "Aye, come inside. I'll put the kettle on," Mr. Campbell said. "Come in from the cold and make yourself at home. You've put a smile on my wife's face. I'm grateful to see it."

Cecily waited for the other choir members to precede her inside the house. Logan walked toward her with his hands tucked inside his sweater pockets. "Thank you, Cecily. I know you're the reason for the choir's visit." He took a sidelong glance at the manor house. "My mother hasn't smiled in days, so this visit means a lot to me. She needed Christmas joy, and here you are, with the entire choir, giving it."

Cecily didn't admit anything, but Abigail was the one he should be thanking. Her sister's inventiveness had encouraged Cecily to bring the Campbell name to Ruth's attention. "I'm glad I made the season brighter for your mother."

He strolled closer. "Will you sing to me? I need Christmas joy, too."

Cecily didn't know what to say, so she didn't say anything.

"Am I making you uncomfortable?" Logan asked.

"It's not like in school when you pulled my hair and placed it inside the inkwell," Cecily said.

"Please forgive me for that wrongdoing. I was young, and boys make foolish mistakes. Let me tell you, lassie, I'd not pull your hair now."

His eyes were bright, twinkling with mischief. He gave her the kind of look that made her wonder... What would he do with his fingers? Would he play with her hair? Surprisingly, she was curious to find out.

"I'm making you uncomfortable. Come inside, Cecily. It would give me pleasure to assist you."

Logan offered his hand, a content expression on his face. Cecily considered the right and wrong of accepting the gesture while staring at his fingers, but then accepted his grasp. A tingle threaded up her fingers and along her arm as Logan escorted her over the stoop and into the Campbell home.

Thank you, Abigail...

LOGAN HAD NEVER BEEN HAPPIER. The evening had tormented him with noise prior to the arrival of the choir. He'd been sitting near the hearth, minding his little sister as she scampered around the room with a doll tucked under her arm, while his rowdier brothers banged their marbles. Logan didn't understand how his parents could ignore the commotion. Smash. Bam. Boom—He needed to escape this madness. Too many people were living inside this house.

And then, when the evening seemed at its darkest, the night sang with promise. An angel's voice, joyful and triumphant, resonated in the air. And now...Cecily's hand on his elbow, this touch belonged on his arm. If luck was on his side, maybe more than music could come from this night. Maybe she'd accept his proposal.

"Father, Mother, I'd like you to meet Cecily Carleton."

His parents perused the placement of Cecily's hand. Perhaps their introspection caused Cecily discomfort as she removed her hand from his elbow. The action left him feeling as if something vital had left. Logan missed her touch. It didn't feel right not having her handhold. He must have made a face for his mother glanced at him as if seeing his heart's intent for the first time, then she scrutinized the woman who might fill the void.

"You have a beautiful voice, my dear."

"Kind of you to say," Cecily said. "I love singing. It's been a pleasure singing for your family."

Mr. Campbell Senior leaned toward Cecily. "You're being modest, lass. You're talented. You put a smile on my wife's face, one this family hasn't seen in days. We're grateful."

"You're welcome, Mr. Campbell," Cecily said. "Mrs. Campbell, I heard you were ill."

Logan's mother glanced at her husband, sighing. "I've had some difficult days, but I'll feel better in a few months."

Logan studied his mother, wondering what her words hinted at, but studying her hand on her belly, the cause of the illness was made more obvious. His suspicion was correct, this wasn't an illness at all. Why hadn't he noticed the evidence before? His mother sickly. Not able to keep much down. Another child? A sibling? Was his mother in the family way, again? His parents hadn't acknowledged the truth, but maybe the truth was difficult to grasp.

Logan observed his siblings spread about the room, seven brothers and one little sister, ranging in ages from four to twenty-four. The family must make space for one more. One more…heaven help him.

MRS. CAMPBELL FROWNED, and in a mother's unhappiness, Cecily recognized the condition. Marriage not only earned a man's affection, but also a physical commitment, which led to the blessings of children. A burden to some households, but she saw that Mr. Campbell had many hands to help him on the farm. But for now, Mrs. Campbell bore the weight.

What could Cecily say to help the situation? To bring hope on a winter night.

"Time heals all discomforts," Cecily said, as a curly-haired girl with stunning brown eyes peered between her parents' legs. Isla wasn't very tall and didn't come much higher than Mr. Campbell's thighs.

Cecily knelt to greet her. "Hello, there. What's your name?"

Isla shook her head and didn't answer, clinging to her parents' legs. That's when Cecily noticed the hazel coloring, hiding in Isla's brown eyes.

"Aren't you a doll," Cecily said, winking.

"I'm not a doll," Isla replied, pouting.

"You're as pretty as a doll, just like your Mama. Did your Mama make your dress?"

Isla glanced at her mother, then at her dress. She nodded, swaying where she stood.

Though Mrs. Campbell smiled at her daughter, Cecily speculated the news of another child hadn't brought happiness, which was reasonable, given Logan's family had ample numbers. Logan stood near his mother, wearing a frown. His brothers ran about the room, their voices loud. The choir stood in various places, conversing. It was clear to Cecily that the family needed joy and the choir's work was not at an end. Maybe one more song to lift their spirits. A children's hymn would be perfect. Cecily began singing:

> All things bright and beautiful,
> All creatures great and small,
> All things wise and wonderful,
> 'Twas God that made them all.

The room yielded to silence. Though Cecily was young and unmarried, she recognized it may not be appropriate to remind the family that some wonders were more precious than others. Especially at Christmas, a season when family celebrated the birth of the Christ child. Maybe two parents needed reminding that *their* unborn child was important, too. Though it may not be appropriate to use their daughter to bring hope, the decision seemed to be working. Isla forgot her shyness and crept toward Cecily. Perhaps a young girl was fascinated by the singer's voice.

She held out her hand and Isla placed her tiny fingers on Cecily's palm.

Each little flower that opens,
Each little bird that sings,

Isla swayed in time to the music, smiling, suddenly entertaining a twirl.

He made their glowing color,
He made their tiny wings.

Cecily glanced at the parents and saw Mrs. Campbell was smiling, weeping as well. "I'm sorry. I meant to bring joy. I didn't mean to make you cry."

Mr. Campbell stood near his wife's side. He didn't seem to know how to respond. Mrs. Campbell wiped at her tears before saying, "Don't worry. You haven't done anything more than help a woman come to her senses." She glanced at her husband. "Will you sing another verse? Isla is dancing and this home needs some happiness."

"What do you think, Isla, with your pretty curls, would you like me to sing again?"

"Aye," Isla said, giggling.

Cecily looked at the choir. "Who will join me, to fill this home with music?"

The choir joined in, and their voices resounded in the great room. It surprised Cecily when Mrs. Campbell began singing, and even Logan. Cecily hadn't known he could sing. It brought joy and enthusiasm into her heart to know she'd given this family the gift of song. The music may have encouraged a tiny bit of peace as well.

He gave us eyes to see them,
And lips that we might tell,
How great is the Almighty,
Who has made all things well[1].

And what was better than joy? The compelling look in Logan's eyes.

CHAPTER EIGHT

When Logan offered to drive Cecily home, she readily accepted. The choral director had voiced an objection, presumably thinking it unwise and inappropriate for an unmarried woman to be chaperoned by an unmarried man. But Cecily had enjoyed sharing the evening with the Campbell family and wasn't ready to leave Logan's presence.

What harm could come from a sleigh ride?

She said goodbye to the choir and was waiting in the house while Logan prepared the sleigh. He came through the doorway, kicking snow off his boots. "It's a terrible night. It's starting to snow. I better get you home, Cecily."

Though Logan had described poor weather, he was smiling. Did his joy stem from the prospect of spending more time with her? She hoped this was the reason. "What woman is ever prepared to journey into freezing weather? If I'm to get home, I suppose we have no choice."

She gazed longingly at the fire in his eyes. They were alone. Mrs. Campbell had left the great room to help the Campbell children prepare for bed.

Logan grasped a quilt. "Then let's go."

They left the house. A draft horse was attached to a sleigh, steam puffing from its nostrils. Logan had placed a thick mattress on the seat. He assisted her into the sleigh, then helped her cover herself with the quilt, and judging by its thickness, it was full of wool batting. She pulled it up to her chin. There was no roof on this sleigh and though she was wearing a fur coat and hat, her face tingled from the frost in the air.

Logan went to the driver's side of the sleigh, gathered the reins, and climbed in beside her. Cecily watched him cover himself with the quilt. "If the chill in the air causes discomfort, I wouldn't mind if you shifted closer to me. We're in for a wintry ride."

Cecily shivered, bearing ice-cold temperatures. She sighed, observing Logan's masculinity; his broad shoulders, massive chest, and strong hands she'd like to touch. Though the invitation appealed to her on a less suggestive level as well, if for no other reason than human warmth.

"My father wouldn't approve." What a silly thing to say, why had she said it?

Logan gave her a meaningful look. "Your father's not in the sleigh."

"That's a cheeky response." His words were true all the same and she was glad of it.

He wasn't quick to respond. Cecily wondered what he was

thinking. The night surrounded them. The earlier brilliance of a starlit sky was gone, hampered by falling snowflakes. She could barely see his face, but as the freezing air penetrated her clothing, she edged closer to him, desiring his warmth. "Promise me you'll be a gentleman?"

He gave the reins a flip, clucked his tongue, and the draft horse bumped forward. "Cecily, I'll be whatever you want me to be."

"Sounds dubious. I don't know what to make of you."

He looked at her; she glimpsed his seriousness. "Can I ask you a personal question?"

"You may ask. I can't guarantee how I'll answer."

"Cecily, how do you feel about me?"

The question caught her by surprise. She should have responded readily, but her thoughts drifted to her father and how he might feel about this Scottish man.

"Logan…"

"It's okay. Don't tell me. Your silence tells me all I need to know."

There was an edge to Logan's voice and Cecily didn't like the discordant tone. The night was frosty enough. She needed to explain. "You don't understand," Cecily said, her heart hurting.

"Help me understand."

"Logan, we're friends," Cecily hedged. Not admitting the problem until she had time to find a solution. "What's there to understand?"

"Our relationship. I want more than friendship." He

paused the sleigh, bringing the draft horse to a stop. "Cecily, I have feelings for you."

Cecily's heart beat a little faster. Father wasn't in the sleigh but his prejudice intruded all the same. She shouldn't permit the intrusion of someone else's bias, but rather should focus on the intention behind Logan's words. The acknowledgement of his feelings meant a lot to her. She wanted his friendship, too.

"Cecily, say something."

"I have…"

"I knew it. The way you looked at me earlier—You care for me, too."

"Logan, it doesn't matter how I feel. You and I, we can't have a relationship."

He grasped her hand, and she welcomed his strength. "Why not?"

Cecily closed her eyes, bearing the weight of her family. "In a word, my father."

"What does your father have to do with this, with us?"

Cecily sighed. "This is impossible. Will you force me to say it?"

"I can't help unless you explain the issue. Just tell me…"

"Wealth and culture," Cecily said with a sigh.

Logan harrumphed. "What? That I don't have as much money as the Carletons? That my heritage is Scottish? What does that have to do with anything?"

Oh god, now she had done it. Cecily hoped she hadn't hurt him. "Our backgrounds have everything to do with it. My father would prefer me to see an English gentleman."

"I may not be English, but I am a gentleman."

"I can see that, but…"

"Does it matter to you?"

Cecily studied Logan, his handsome face. The snowflakes fluttered between them. He squeezed her fingers. It felt right being this close. Why was she permitting her father's opinion to intrude on her wants and needs? Where was her courage hiding? "To me, it's not about our history, not even our backgrounds. Whether you were a prince or a pauper, it wouldn't matter to me."

"Do birds ask their parents' opinions before selecting a partner? I think not. Fathers should mind their own business. They have no say in their children's partners."

"Yes, well, I agree with you in theory. But Father considers his children as more of an investment."

"That's terrible; he doesn't own you. What do you want, Cecily? The decision should be yours to make."

She eyed Logan, yearning for him as if his strength could save her from life's difficult moments. But she agreed with him to a point, important decisions should be hers to make, especially those that affected the choosing of a partner.

In this moment, with this man sitting beside her who she'd had a crush on since forever, suddenly she didn't care for parental opinion. The chill in the air didn't affect her as much. The snowflakes wafting between them helped her to smile. Logan squeezed her hand. She looked upward, gazing into his eyes. "If it were my choice to make, I'd welcome more time with you, to find out…" what she already knew. Logan Campbell satisfied her heart's desire.

"If we're compatible?" Logan asked, leaning toward her. A pleasant look on his face. He removed his glove and wiped a crystallized flake from her cheek.

Cecily shivered. Not from the chill in the air but from his close proximity. They were compatible all right. Logan sat near her, holding her hand. Her heart said yes, her lips parted and she said, "No."

"What, then?"

"I'm sorry, Logan. Though I do have feelings for you, I can't go against my parents' wishes. It wouldn't be right. I honestly don't know what to do."

"You haven't talked to your parents to find out if they would object." He sighed, then released her hand. He flicked the reins and encouraged the draft horse to a trot. Cecily didn't speak as they slid across the fields, dashing through the snow.

"Would you court me?" Logan asked, "if you were free to do so?"

There seemed little point in lying, as Cecily had already confessed the truth. "I would, but how could I? You couldn't very well drive up to Carleton House. Father might challenge you. I'm worried about the conflict that could take place."

"What conflict? A duel? Those days are long past," Logan said. "You're shivering up a storm. Cecily, come closer to me."

"Didn't you hear me? I wouldn't want anything to happen to you."

"I sure did," he said, lifting his arm. "The problem isn't

that you won't consider a relationship with me, but how we can spend time together in an appropriate way."

She merged with the space between them, tucked closer to his side. He was tall, solid, woodsmoke drifted from him. It felt good being this close, even though she didn't know how they'd manage a relationship.

"What are you suggesting?" Cecily asked hopefully. She didn't have the answers. Maybe he did.

"Leave this problem with me," Logan replied, managing the reins. "I have an idea. I'll find a way to approach your father, too."

CHAPTER NINE

The second Sunday of Advent arrived with the theme of peace. When Cecily walked into the church sanctuary for choir practice, she least expected to find Logan sitting in the choral loft. He stared at her in a 'Yes I Can' kind of way, his intrepid look causing her mind to spin and her spine to tingle with awareness while standing in the center aisle.

Why was Logan here? And more importantly, what were his intentions? She reacted, her face heating, her forehead furrowing, and Logan…that rascal, studied her in a playful, humorous way.

Cecily didn't want to make a spectacle of herself, so gave Logan a dazed look and then took a seat beside him. Other choir members had yet to join them.

"Won't you say hello?" Logan asked, seeming pleased with himself.

Cecily shook her head. "Mr. Campbell, why are you here?"

"Isn't it obvious? I'm joining the choir."

Cecily stared into his gorgeous hazel eyes, forgetting the other parishioners. Logan seemed happy with his decision. To be in the choir or be in her company? "I didn't know you could sing."

"Weren't you listening to me the other night? I have some musical talent. We should practice together sometime. Maybe Ruth could give us a duet."

Cecily wondered where they might practice if they were ever afforded the opportunity to sing together. The hunter's cabin came to mind.

"Shh…" Cecily whispered near his ear. "Emmaline is a gossip. She'll tell Margaret, Margaret will tell Lucy, and before you know it…my mother will know you've joined the choir."

Logan laughed out loud. "You can't keep it a secret. Your mother and sister will find out next Sunday, since I'll be sitting right beside you."

"Right beside me?" Cecily asked, fretting. "Oh, joy." The thought of seeing Logan again, this Sunday, next Sunday— every Sunday, tickled her with happiness. This surprising moment was the best part of her day.

However, Logan's decision might inspire too much curiosity, namely her mother's. She might question if a relationship was evolving between the Campbells' eldest son and the Carletons' eldest daughter. Though quite suddenly, other people's opinions didn't matter. She sat in a place of peace. She couldn't stop smiling, even giggling. *Logan's here, he's beside me.* His nearness gave her pleasure.

Logan smiled. "I knew you'd be happy to see me."

"I am, though I wonder, how will my family respond to the new choir member?"

Truer words had never been spoken. Cecily adored having Logan here, but she couldn't predict her mother's reaction. Father didn't attend Sunday service, but if her mother told him, what then? The thought caused her heart to constrict. Her parents were bound to ask questions, especially if Abigail inadvertently blurted the truth. She wanted to be bold like Logan.

"They'll love my singing voice as much as my mother does," Logan said. "Tell them she forced me to try out for the position and Ruth couldn't reject the new singer."

"In truth, she never turns anyone away. It's difficult coming across good talent." Cecily's brows rose with the admission. "Though I never suspected your talent. You're a resourceful man, Logan Campbell. I underestimated you."

"I'm a man on a mission."

"To find a wife? I think not. You just want me in your sleigh again."

He nudged her arm. "I'm available after practice?" Logan replied suggestively. "Your family left after the service. I was planning on offering you a ride home."

"You have it all planned."

"Not everything. Not yet, but I'm working on it."

A CHEER WENT up when Ruth announced that Logan had joined the choir. Male members were difficult to find and Logan was a tenor. Cecily knew he had an ulterior motive. He probably couldn't even sing. But as the practice began and the choir's voices rose in song, her assessment was proven wrong.

Cecily listened to the eloquent tone in Logan's voice, his smooth and connected vocal tones and breathy whispers. An angel was singing near her, his intonation potent and pleasing to the ear. Transfixed by his proximity as well as his voice, Cecily lost her place. Logan winked at her, pointing at the sheet music, enabling her to take up the song again.

If Logan hadn't fascinated Cecily before, he held her rapt attention now that they had more in common than mutual attraction. To sing a duet with him would be amazing.

Ruth seemed impressed with the new choir member as well. She was all smiles. "Where have you been hiding?" she asked, holding her baton, "and more importantly, can I convince you to remain a member?"

"I'd like to, but I'm not sure of my voice. Is it strong enough? Does it harmonize well with the other singers? The other members have talent, especially Cecily. I'm only an average singer."

It wasn't true. There was nothing average about Logan, but Cecily didn't say so.

"You're being modest. Let me assure you, you'll fit in well here," Ruth said. "We're glad to have you, aren't we choir?"

No one said much. Cecily wasn't close to the other choir members. They were either shy, or as she suspected, more envious of her talent and family name. Even so, she enjoyed singing with them.

Later during a break, Cecily said, "You have a gift, you can sing."

"My mother enjoys my singing. In fact, she's the one who suggested I join the choir. Though I suspect she had an ulterior motive."

"Me?" Cecily's eyebrows rose with the question.

"I may have told her about my intentions toward you."

"Really?" Cecily said, nibbling at her lip. She admired his unflinching confidence. That he'd be so gallant as to tell his mother about this lady in the choir. She wished she could do the same with her family. "How does Mrs. Campbell feel about me?"

"You made an impression the other evening, which is why she came to the service this morning," Logan said. "Finally, there's peace in our house. It's all because of you."

Cecily swallowed. That sounded positive. Perhaps a good impression had been made. "I'm glad I could help. I'll thank your mother for her suggestion."

"You can thank her next week. Though she occupied a pew this morning, she wasn't in church to hear me, or even listen to the minister's sermon."

"Really? If not her son's singing voice, then what?"

Logan nudged Cecily's arm. "You, Cecily. My mother wants to hear you sing again."

Cecily's eyes widened as she recognized that Mrs. Campbell had wanted more than to listen to her sing. She had watched her, staring at her intently during the service. She'd felt the intensity of the look. For what reason? To hear her singing voice or discern if the English girl was a good fit for her son? "That's a lot of pressure."

"Yes, well, it doesn't matter how old a son gets, a mother wants to know her son has chosen the right woman."

Cecily squirmed on her chair. *Chosen the right woman?* How should she respond to such news? What should she do to prove her worth? It was enough to cope with the challenges of her own family as she suspected a smooth singing voice wasn't a strong enough ability for any mother's son.

"Would your mother's opinion change anything?" Cecily asked.

"No. She doesn't have any say in the matter. I know what I want."

Cecily nodded. "I do, too."

One factor was apparent; their relationship had taken a curious shift, and family opinion wasn't all that mattered.

CHAPTER TEN

John Carleton had achieved financial success by breeding the best equestrian horses. A top entertainment for the upper class, everyone desired a Carleton horse as many won at the racetrack. Cecily suspected her father valued his horses more than his children. The stable better occupied than their house. It surprised her he'd chosen to join his family for Sunday's dinner.

But worry marred his forehead. He wore his anxiety on his face, his demeanor wrinkling into a perpetual frown. His hard look must have something to do with the horses.

John cleared his voice. "I noticed someone dropped you off at the house earlier, Cecily."

An underlying tick in his tone gave him an edge. Cecily recognized the grilling about to come and stabbed at a piece of meat, searching for patience and wisdom while giving her sister a coy look. "Oh yes...after the choir practice, Mr. Campbell offered a ride."

"The senior Campbell, or Logan, the eldest son?"

Cecily chewed the goose meat thoughtfully, glancing at him. "Logan. He joined the choir recently, and since we're neighbors, he offered me a ride. His father rarely attends church."

"Is that so? Didn't know anyone in the Campbell family had talent."

Cecily gave him a weary smile that didn't reach her eyes. The comment was impertinent and rude, especially given Logan's veterinary skills. "Is there something inappropriate with the invite?"

"Your mother hasn't taught you proper manners." He raised his eyes, studying her seriously. Cecily felt like an ant under a magnifying glass.

"Unchaperoned?" Father asked.

"Of course not. Mrs. Campbell accompanied us, her daughter, Isla, as well. She's an adorable child, though the tiny bird either tweeted or sang Christmas carols."

"Oh? What did you talk about?"

Cecily didn't appreciate the grilling. Her father was intruding in her personal life, her personal space, a place he had no right to occupy. She wished she didn't live in this impersonal house anymore. She felt like a faceless person talking to an invasive pest.

"Well…it was difficult having a conversation with Isla in the sleigh. You know how children can be, they're like songbirds. They never stop singing."

Not that her father understood anything about young children or even a family scene that was commonplace for a lower-class family. He'd rarely seen his daughters while they were youngsters, preferring to hide them away with the nanny. Only now did his children join their parents at the table, now that she and Abigail were adults.

"Did the minister give a good sermon?"

Cecily sighed, irritated by the probing. "It was dull and dry if you must know, and not very inspiring. He talked about the Nativity as it relates to the Christ child, and peace, making the comparison between darkness and light."

Her father should have joined her mother and sister at the service. The Advent sermons would benefit him, especially the peace sermons.

"Did you sing?"

"The choir sang one choral piece and several hymns. Had you been in attendance you'd have enjoyed *O Come, all ye Faithful,* " Cecily said, hoping to change the topic. "I'm sure you're grateful the temperature has improved. Must make it easier while providing care for the horses."

Her tactful approach achieved nothing. Father didn't alter his stance.

"Cecily, is there something you're not telling me?"

Cecily squeezed her fork a little too tight. "What are you suggesting, Papa?"

"The real reason Mrs. Campbell went to church?"

"I told you, to hear us sing."

"You and who?"

"For heaven's sake," Mrs. Carleton said, seeming frustrated by the badgering, "would you stop. Skye came to hear her son. As far as I can tell, Logan has a nice voice, though it was difficult to know. Margaret doesn't have an ear for song and sings louder than everyone else."

"Cecily, something doesn't feel right. Tell me the truth. Why were you in the Campbell sleigh?"

"For heaven's sake, Papa, you tell me. Is there something wrong with Mr. Campbell giving me a ride? Logan is our neighbor. He's a gifted veterinary surgeon. If you asked him, he'd assist you with the horses. That is, if you'll let a poorer man near the stable."

Father succumbed to silence, either considering her words or a veterinary surgeon's skills. Whatever problem her father faced, his real issue arose from more than their current conversation.

"He's a Scot and a poorer man." Father's temperament changed. He sounded like a dog gnawing on a bone. "If he's interested in you, we must put a stop to it."

Cecily felt her cheeks heating. She hadn't expected a confrontation. She wanted to respond in an insolent way, by making a rude impertinent comment as ill-mannered as the conversation her father orchestrated, no different than Ruth directing the choir, but by the way he was analyzing her, the conversation needed to end and as quickly as possible.

"Has the younger Mr. Campbell spoken to you? Offended you in some way? There must be a reason that a sleigh ride is concerning."

"Would you tell me…"

"Of course, Papa. You're my father."

He nodded, accepting her words. The dinner continued, but Cecily fretted, feeling uneasy. She would lie to protect her relationship with Logan. Abigail glanced at her then, appearing discouraged, too.

Though her father's position was clear, it didn't change anything for Cecily. She had feelings for Logan and he had feelings for her. She supposed they could see each other secretly, though accepting another ride might be problematic. Her father would scrutinize her every move.

Cecily despaired. She couldn't admit her feelings to her parents. Not yet, anyway. The truth must remain hidden. The minister's sermon came to mind…darkness and light. Father was living in a world of perpetual darkness, ignorance at the very least. How could she give him light? Christmas light?

Cecily glanced at her mother in a hopeful way, thinking she might have to talk to her about the situation, but she wouldn't broach the subject while in her father's company. A mother daughter conversation should happen in the near future.

LILLIAN CARLETON HAD a gentler soul than her husband. A practical woman, she was accustomed to being alone in her marriage and didn't want the same frustration for her daughter. It was a mother's responsibility to guide her children and keep them safe.

She'd noticed sensitivity in Cecily's eyes. A distant truth. A hidden resolve. Lillian recognized that look for what it was. Desire. Logan was an attractive man. A mother understood why Cecily might be charmed by him.

If her suspicions were proven correct, Cecily should understand where desire could take a woman if she chose to court a poorer man's son. It was necessary for them to talk privately. Lillian didn't want her husband privy to the conversation.

She waited until John was asleep and snoring, then left their bed to speak to Cecily.

CECILY WAS READING when the door to her bedchamber slid open. Mama came into the room wearing her nightclothes and carrying a lantern. Seeing her mother in the bedroom at this late hour was surprising. Why was she here?

"Mama?"

"Shh…" Her mother placed her finger on her lips, then motioned for Cecily to follow. She placed the book on the side table and climbed out of bed. Then reached for a wrap and blew out the flame in the oil lamp. What did her mother want?

Lillian didn't say a word as mother and daughter walked along the hallway and then down a narrow flight of stairs into the kitchen.

"What is it? Why are we sneaking around the house at this late hour?"

"We need to talk. A place where your father won't disturb us," Lillian said. "Earlier at dinner, you lied to your parents. I'm hoping you'll be more honest with your mother."

"About what?"

"Keep your voice down," Lillian said, whispering. "We don't want to awaken your father."

Cecily pondered her mother's comment, supposing whatever concern that had brought her into the bedchamber, she didn't want the head of the household included in the conversation. Concerned, Cecily sat on a chair at the kitchen table. She pulled her wrap tighter around herself, feeling cold, and waited for her mother to speak.

"A mother knows when their children are lying and picks up on the truth faster than a father could ever guess."

Cecily glanced at her warily. "What do you think I'm lying about?"

"Your friendship with Logan. You sat beside each other at church today. Your eyes lit up. You smiled every time you looked at him, but I didn't suspect anything until you lied to your father."

Cecily shook her head. "There isn't a relationship."

"Cecily…"

"No, Mama, Logan and I are only friends."

Mother studied her carefully. Cecily squirmed on her chair while bearing the scrutiny. "Is this the truth?"

Cecily stared at her, not wanting to admit anything. Soft lantern light illuminated the concern on her mother's face as she patiently waited for a response. Cecily warred with herself. To be honest or dishonest? But she supposed her mother would find out eventually. Lies had a way of coming out.

"What if it were true?" Cecily asked. "How would you

respond to news that your daughter is lovesick over a farmer's son?"

"I'd be worried for you."

"That's a terrible thing to say. I'm your daughter. Why can't you support me?"

"I'm your mother. It's not my job to please you. It's my responsibility to remind you what you'd be giving up if you chose a farmer's son." Lillian placed the oil lamp she'd been carrying on the table and a took a seat. "Mr. Campbell does not have the wherewithal to support you in the manner you're accustomed to living."

Cecily thought about her mother's remark. The truth hung in the air between them. She lived a grand lifestyle. Had everything a woman could want and more. Yet money couldn't buy everything. What was she to do when her heart desired Logan? Cecily said honestly, "Does the size of the house matter? Is the amount of money in a man's pocket important? What about love, Mama?"

Her mother frowned, but Cecily didn't know that Lillian's disappointment had nothing to do with her daughter. "I can't answer the question about who *you* should love. Only you can answer that."

"Then why are we here?"

"I didn't bring you to the kitchen to lecture you or tell you how to live your life. Only to present the facts. Love might keep your bed warm at night, but it doesn't pay the bills," she said, unsmiling.

"Logan and I are not seeing each other."

"We're having this conversation because I know what you want. I can see it in your eyes."

Cecily knew what she wanted as well. She just didn't know if she had the courage to voice it openly. "What do I want?"

"You lied."

"Why are you so certain?"

"Skye may have chaperoned a couple in the family sleigh this past Sunday, but she didn't the previous week after a certain choir visit to the Campbell property."

Cecily sucked in a shocked breath. How had mother learned about the visit? Maybe Ruth, or some other busybody in the choir?

"Will you tell Father?"

"No, I won't. This conversation is between you and me. And furthermore, whether you see Logan or not, that is your decision to make, not mine, and certainly not your father's."

"Will you support me?"

Her mother sighed. "I've always supported you, but I can't help unless you tell me the truth. Are you seeing Logan Campbell?"

Cecily swallowed. "I want to. He's asked me."

"You have a lot to consider. Mind your decision with care, and don't make a choice based on emotion," Lillian said wistfully. "I have no quarrel with the man himself. I do hear whispers of conversation from other congregants who have led me to believe that Logan Campbell is a good and honest man, an animal whisperer...even so, a poorer man."

What could Cecily say to such a comment? Her mother

wasn't exactly supporting her, wasn't defending her position either, but rather just pointing out the facts.

When Cecily returned to her bedchamber, she laid on her bed, unable to sleep, bearing a heavy conscience.

What should she do?

Why was life so difficult?

If only the world was a simpler place where money and social class didn't matter. Maybe then she'd be free to choose the partner who would ultimately make her happier.

CHAPTER ELEVEN

Intent on meeting Logan, Cecily urged the mare along her family's laneway. She barely noticed the marine blue sky, the horses in the snow-covered field, or poplar trees lining the edges of their land.

Her thoughts were heavy; her nerves tattered and torn. Her mother had only made her feelings for Logan more difficult to accept. Did the advice change anything? Certainly not her love for a farmer's son. The mare raised her ears even before Cecily heard the other horse. When she saw Logan, she tried to smile, but she'd never been good about concealing her sadness.

"What's wrong?" Logan asked as he drew nearer.

Cecily glanced at the field, urging the mare to a stop. "Logan, why is life so difficult?"

He rode closer and studied her in a way that made her uneasy, perusing her more than the question. "Lass, life isn't difficult, people make it difficult."

Cecily stared at Logan, perceiving his strength and kindness. "To hear you speak, one might question if a person has cause to worry."

Logan's eyebrows rose. "Whatever it is, you can tell me."

Cecily's mare hoofed forward slightly. "To be frank, I had a conversation with my mother. She's discovered we have a relationship."

Logan grinned, giving her a half-smile. Her admission seemed to intrigue him. "Do we? You haven't agreed to a partnership yet."

"I told her as much, but she saw through the lie." Logan's grin widened at the admission. "What about this makes you happy?"

"It's nothing. It pleases me to know you want what I want."

"Well, I thought I was accepting of the prospect, but my mother reminded me of our class situations."

Logan frowned. "And does this change things for you, or alter your feelings for me? The fact that I'm a farmer and you're a high society kind of gal?"

His eyebrows rose with the question. Did two ways of life change anything for her? Not really. His heart still beckoned her heart.

"You can't deny we have two *very* different lifestyles," Cecily said, hoping she hadn't caused offense. "I'm not telling you everything my mother revealed, but she made some valid points."

"Did the conversation cause you to question your feelings for me?"

Cecily studied Logan on his horse while he waited for her response. His hands held tight to the reins, maybe too tight. The worry in her heart mirrored in his eyes. "Certainly not anything to do with your character. More so about how you would provide for me. As I said before, life is difficult."

Logan climbed down from his horse and approached her. He reached for her, his strong hands grasping her waist. She sighed as he helped her dismount. "Let's walk for a bit, lass. Movement helps me think better."

"All right."

He grasped her horse's reins and they continued up the trail that wound around a frozen lake. "Why has your mother's conversation upset you? Be honest with me, I can take it."

Cecily gave Logan a sidelong glance. "Well, it's made me question if what I want best serves my needs. After all, you and I, we come from two different classes of people."

He gave a nervous laugh. "I agree with what you're saying to a point. I'm a simple man with simple priorities, but I assure you, I can provide for a wife and probably better than your parents know. But tell me, what do you want from life? What do you expect from me?"

Cecily paused, gazing into his eyes. The mare nickered behind her. "I don't know. I suppose a cheerful home, a family to cherish, a husband to love. When I look at you...I cannot think. My pulse races, my face flushes, I don't know what to say."

He smiled at this news. "I hardly know what to say

hearing you speak such tender words. Fills my head with pride, my heart with happiness to hear it."

Cecily blushed. "I'm glad it means something to you."

"Lassie…I can give you a happy home. I look at you and see everything I've always wanted. The woman I want to see when I open my eyes in the morning. The wife I want to hold when closing my eyes at the end of the day. I want to share my life with you."

"I'm flattered. You make the time shared between two people sound simple."

He grasped her shoulder. A small gesture that projected his care. "When it comes right down to it, life is simple. Don't you want the same?" When he released his tender embrace, she certainly wanted it back.

Cecily sighed. "I'm confused, Logan. There's much to consider. How would we spend our time in between the daylight hours?"

They continued walking along the trail.

"If your concern comes from how a couple would manage their time, we wouldn't be having this conversation. Your mother must have pointed out that I'm a farmer. That you'll wrestle with livestock instead of money. Get dirty instead of singing or playing the piano. We probably shouldn't be talking to each other."

Cecily paused on the pathway, facing Logan. "I want to talk to you." Cecily appealed to him. "I don't mind challenging work and I'm capable of learning. I'll feed the chickens. I'll whisper to the animals, but I can't give you my hand without talking things through," she said, frowning.

"How would we live?" Logan snickered, as if she'd said something funny.

"Somehow, I can't picture it, you in your fancy dress, whispering to the animals." He left her then and led both horses to a nearby tree. He knotted their reins to the trunk and then returned to her. "How do you want to live, Miss Carleton? I suspect you'd want a grand home to suit your grand lifestyle."

Cecily paused to think about his statement, wondering if there was judgment in it. But Logan waited for her to respond. She said, "I would like a comfortable home. I've already voiced this."

"I can give you comfort. Come this way."

Logan extended his gloved hand and Cecily grasped it without hesitation. Together, they left the main trail and tramped across a field laden with snow. She didn't understand his reasoning, but permitted his escort without questioning the motive, across frozen ground with a good view of an equally frozen lake. Side by side, they walked together, trekking through the snowfall and the left-behind fodder of cut hay.

"Logan, what are you trying to prove with this exercise?" she asked, protesting. "The snow is cold. It's climbing my legs."

He gave her a determined look. "This is good land. It borders your family's property as well as mine. We could build a house here. As big as you want. I'm handy with carpentry tools and my father would help. Maybe the neighbors would pitch in as they like me well enough." He smiled at her then. "My brothers will pound the nails if I ask them. Hell, to give you the grandest house money can buy, I'll hire the entire town. How many rooms do you want?"

Logan released his hold. She watched him kicking a straight line through the snow. "I'd like a breezeway at the front entrance."

"Done," he said, creating a square area in the snow. "What else?"

Cecily stepped closer to him. "A drawing room on the right, a study on the left."

Logan kicked at the snow, fashioning these imaginary rooms, too. "There, you have them."

Cecily approached the imaginary breezeway and passed through it. Logan hadn't made a hallway in between the two rooms, so she imagined that one was already in place. "Could we have a dining room?"

"Anything your heart desires."

Cecily forgot her worries and joy lit her face as she watched Logan going through his paces. She knew his effort wasn't real. This construction site was merely a field of snow and brilliant sunlight with a maze of trenches that Logan had constructed with his booted feet. But in her mind, she imagined a house and a real future taking shape.

Her future. His Future. Their future together?

"A kitchen at the back of the house," Cecily said, marching through the snow, now assisting with creating the perimeter of the house.

Logan joined her in their imaginary kitchen. "You'll need a pantry for the preserves."

Cecily's feet were getting cold, but she didn't think about

herself while watching Logan work. He pivoted, looking at her.

"I don't know what your favorite foods are," Cecily said. "Would we hire a cook, or would we be too poor to afford a servant in our home?"

There it was. The question that caused Logan to pause in his imaginary build. He placed his hands on his hips. He sighed. "Don't look so devastated. I'm a simple man with simple tastes. If you don't know how to cook, we'll eat cheese and bread."

"I have some ability in the kitchen, gratefully nanny thought it was important for the Carleton girls to have culinary skills, but I don't cook often. Do you want a wife who has limited abilities?"

He came toward her and embraced her gloved hands in his own, his facial expression earnest. "Nothing is insurmountable. Even I have subjects to learn. I'd rather ask a more important question."

"What?"

"Our bedroom. Where should it be located?"

How should she respond? She studied his heartfelt expression, the question hanging in the air between them as he squeezed her hand, patiently waiting for a reply. She didn't speak.

"Do you want to share a bedroom, lass?"

Cecily swallowed. The gap between them grew wider. She released his hand and took a full step backward. "I can't answer that right now."

"You can't, or you won't."

"You need to give me more time."

He grasped her hand again. "What about the two of us and the life we could live if there were no society strictures forcing us apart. There are no rules to any one lifestyle. Would you say yes, then? Be honest."

Cecily took a deep breath. Her lower lip quivered. If she didn't control her emotions, she would cry. "I want you now, Logan. This imaginary home and the real one we would build together. I want it all. Even the bedroom."

"You want me?"

Logan seemed surprised by her admission. Cecily bridged the gap between them and moved closer to his strength. "Yes, I want you."

Logan pulled her into his arms and she nestled against his chest willingly. Every part of her vibrated with the need to be held. The need to be loved. "Can I kiss you?" Logan asked.

Cecily looked upward then, seeing the naked desire in Logan's eyes. She nodded, and he kissed her. Their first caress was everything she'd hoped a kiss might be. Soft and sweet. She could barely breathe, her heartbeat was racing. The wind softly whispered against her face, but she barely felt it. If it hadn't been necessary to return home, she would have kissed him for the entire afternoon.

Logan leaned against her forehead. He removed his gloves and stroked her cheek. His fingers were cold. She tingled with awareness.

"Does this mean we're courting, Cecily?"

She laid her head against his chest. She smiled. "Yes, well, since we're planning our first home, it seems like a natural next step."

Logan kissed her forehead. Though Cecily enjoyed the kiss as much as the embrace, she wondered how her parents would react or whether she'd tell them. Eventually, she'd have to face the consequences of this decision.

"Being with you is the easy part," Cecily said, her hand on his chest. "My only worry is how my parents will accept us."

"Don't worry," Logan said, squeezing her fingers. "I'll take care of you. Whatever must be faced, we'll face it together."

Cecily wished life was simpler, yet she was grateful for Logan's strength and confidence in the matter. At this moment, he was her rock. Nothing in this world was more important than his tenderness. Her parents couldn't embrace her in this way.

CHAPTER TWELVE

ogan had hoped some time would pass before a face-to-face encounter with Cecily's father, but a meeting had come sooner than expected. A summons had come early Sunday morning, requesting his presence at his earliest convenience.

What did John want? Did this plea have anything to do with his relationship with Cecily?

Whatever the reason, responding to the request meant he'd miss the church service and possibly the choir practice as well. Logan might not see Cecily today and the thought of not seeing her aggrieved him. Everything focused on the reason for this visit and the time required to address the issue.

Could it be about the Carleton horses? If so, an animal's health took precedence. He'd become known as somewhat of an animal whisperer. Local farmers called on him when their animals were ill. Though if a horse was unwell, this would be the first time John had called on his veterinary services.

Carrying his veterinary bag, just in case, Logan met John near the stable's entrance: a rectangular timber-framed building. Logan didn't pay much attention to the richness of the structure or the gabled roof. The only standing that mattered to him, in places such as this, centered on animal health and a secure shelter when not in the pasture.

"Good morning," he said, shaking John's hand. "I came as soon as I could. What can I do for you?"

"One of my horses needs care," John said, his tone serious. "I'm not sure if you're aware of my business."

Holding his bag, Logan breathed a sigh of relief. His visit had nothing to do with him or Cecily. He studied John Carleton, gauging his apprehension more so than his appearance. Dressed for a ride rather than wintry weather, he wore a bowler hat and a plaid sack suit. John seemed uneasy. He glanced at the stable's double door, seeming eager to usher him through the entrance.

"Who hasn't heard of you. Your family is famous in Essex, but that's not why you asked me here."

"No, of course not," John said, studying him in a shrewd manner. He moved toward the doorway. "Something's been off with one of my horses. A mare's been acting up. I can't put my finger on what the problem might be. My regular vet has returned to England."

"Explains why I've been busy." Logan wasn't offended to come in second place. He shifted his focus to an ill horse. "Take me to her."

They passed through the pitching door. Logan followed

John as they walked along a cobblestoned aisle toward a stall near the back of the stable.

"In case she's ill, I've separated her from the rest of the horses."

Logan moved closer to the stall. "That's good. What's her name?"

"Lady Luck. She's a favorite. Just look at her…perfect conformation, gorgeous chestnut coloring. She's carrying an important foal." John glanced at him, giving him a pointed look. "I can't afford for her to be sick."

Logan observed Lady Luck from a distance, studying her general behavior and stance. Though her eyes were open, they seemed dull and unfocused. Her stretched neck concerned him. "Looks safe to go inside. Will she tolerate a physical exam?"

"She's been good with the handler. Good with me, too."

"Then open the gate."

John opened the gate and Logan went inside the stall.

Though the horse peered at him, she didn't shift her head. "Easy, girl," Logan said, placing his bag on the stall's floor. He took a closer look. He frowned.

John leaned against the stall. He fingered his hat. "She seems depressed to me. She's lying down more than usual. Seems restless most days, too. Gets up, circles the stall, lies back down."

"Nothing to be concerned about. It's a common behavior prior to giving birth," Logan said. "It's obvious she's in foal." Logan knelt near her hind legs. Though Lady Luck quivered, she accepted his touch. "No sign of udder distention or milk in the teats." He stood and checked her hind end.

"Do you think she's losing the foal?" John asked with a grimace. "It's not due until spring."

Logan glanced at John, seeing the disquiet in his eyes. "Other than restlessness, there's no indication she's laboring. Though she might be trying to shift the foal."

Logan did a general examination, looking for reasons for ill health. Lady Luck tolerated his touch; he paid attention to her eyes, mouth, nose, and other areas, such as her forelimbs and hind limbs. He felt along her abdomen. "Is it possible she has colic?"

Logan heard John sigh. "She's eating less, but she's eating. I've considered it."

"Has she had time out of the stall? Is she getting exercise?"

"I haven't had the horses in the pasture given the recent weather. Too cold and too much snow. And now that she's ill…"

"It's okay, John, you're doing everything you can," Logan said, offering his support. "You've made the right decision. It's best to keep her separated from the other horses. What have you been feeding her?"

"Mostly hay, some oats."

"I'd recommend adding turnip to the feed," Logan said, facing John. "Cold weather can be hard on horses. Adding root vegetables to the diet can help them during the winter months. Not only for this girl, but for all your horses. Boil them, chop them up, and mix them into the chaff."

"I'll do that if I can find any."

"We had a good crop this year. We grow as much as we can. We never know who's going to need help. We can spare some."

John nodded. "I'd be grateful to make a purchase." His expression returned to concern. "Can you tell what's wrong with Lady Luck?"

Logan scratched his head. "Hard to say. The horse could be depressed, could be uncomfortable given her pregnancy, but an underlying condition might be the reason as well. Nutrition could be off. Too much of one feed, not enough of another. We've suffered a recent cold snap. Winter in these parts requires different care for different animals."

The horse's behavior concerned Logan, particularly the getting up and going down restlessness while circling the stall. The horse could be losing her foal, but there was no point in telling John. The news would only add to his worry.

"There's many days I wish I'd stayed in England," John said, sighing. "It's too cold here. There's fewer problems in the homeland." He eyed him. "You know more than I expected you would."

"I have training."

"Been to school?"

Logan's brow rose. "The Ontario Veterinary College. I'm passionate about helping animals."

John nodded. "That's what I've heard. It's why I asked you here. Do you have other advice for me? Anything at all?"

"Keep an eye on Lady Luck. Let me know if anything changes."

"I'd be grateful if you'd check on her again."

"I can do that. In the meantime, add turnips to the mix at the end of the day. Hydration is important. Access to clean water and a salt block."

"You don't mess around."

Logan rubbed the horse's neck, worrying, wondering if there could be something more. He reached for his bag.

John opened the gate and Logan left the stall. He moved to walk along the aisle, but John remained where he was standing, his focus on the horse. The fear in his eyes, the way he quietly assessed her, as if he knew in his gut that something was terribly wrong. This manly act told Logan that John cared for his horse.

"I hope she's not losing the foal," John said, closing the gate.

Logan realized John feared this outcome more than anything else. "Let's not concern ourselves with the worst. Try to focus on the positive. How long have you had her?"

They walked along the aisle.

"Only a few months. She was a healthy spirited filly at first. This change worries me."

Logan scratched his head. "It could be an illness, hard to know at this point. I'd recommend a daily walk to ease her anxiety." Such an activity would benefit the animal and its anxious master. "When the weather improves, putting her in the pasture would benefit her as well, giving her the opportunity to forage."

"I appreciate your advice."

Logan paused at the entrance to the stable. "John, have you vaccinated your horses?"

"I believe so."

"That doesn't sound convincing."

"She came with papers."

"John, you should consider vaccinating your horses, especially Lady Luck, in case she's come in contact with a bat or some other rabid animal."

"Do you think she has rabies?" A look of horror passed across John's face.

That look told Logan a lot about this man. His horses were more than a means of income. He loved them. Logan wanted to alleviate the worry if he could.

"Other than depression, she's not showing signs of rabies. No fever, no muscle weakness. No psychological signs. Though the restlessness concerns me. Better to vaccinate, just in case, rather than lose your horse later."

John nodded. "I'd like you to do it as soon as possible."

Logan was impressed that John supported the suggestion without asking him questions about the benefits or drawbacks of vaccines. Other men wouldn't make the same choice.

"I'll come back later today. I need to collect the vaccine. I'll bring a load of turnips at the same time."

"How much will the vaccine cost?"

"No more expensive than your bowler hat, but she'll need four doses."

John shook his head. "Okay, please do it."

As Logan left the Carleton residence, he wondered what

Cecily was afraid of. He'd met many people in this country while checking on their animals' welfare and one thing was for sure, a man who took care of his horses took care of his family, too. Maybe the way to John's heart was through his horses.

The third Sunday of Advent should have brightened Cecily's spirits. The congregation was about to celebrate joy. But as the start time for the service came closer and closer, her mood tempered toward regret.

Where was Logan? Why hadn't he arrived yet?

The congregants drifted into the sanctuary; happy couples, playful children, enthusiastic seniors, everyone excited to worship together as a community. They talked in the pews, the aisle, even at the front entrance. *Peace be with you...*

They'd come to hear the minister's message, to praise, to listen to sweet melodies singing from the choir. Cecily had another calling. One that hearkened to her heart and soul. *Love.* To see her love and hear the throaty rumble of his voice. Though inside this spiritual place, her heartfelt desires seemed somewhat selfish.

Yet up until the very last minute, just moments before the service began, she greedily watched for one ginger-haired gentleman to pass through the doorway. Much to her disappointment, he didn't make it on time and the choir sang without him.

When the time came for the choir's anthem, her voice wasn't as strong. Not nearly as sweet. She closed her eyes, envisioning his strength, his touch, missing him, then carried on in a lukewarm way, her voice dull and uninspiring, singing songs of joy that were not as joyful without Logan.

CECILY ASSUMED Logan wouldn't attend the choir practice either, so was surprised when he entered the sanctuary. Her face lit up, seeing him in the center aisle. She took a deep breath, gazing at him as if she hadn't seen him in days. He paced forward and sat down beside her. "I'm sorry I'm late. Did you miss me? Are you happy to see me?"

Joy filled her heart. She smiled. "I missed you at the service. What happened?"

His brows rose. "You know what they say, what can go wrong will go wrong. A horse required my veterinary skills."

"I'm sorry to hear it. Anyone I know?"

"Aye, surprisingly, one of your father's horses."

"That is surprising," Cecily said, making a face. Logan and her father in the same stable? That was difficult to imagine. What did it suggest?

"Has he asked for your help before?"

"No, but it's my job to oversee animal care. Your father owns superb horses."

Cecily couldn't comprehend that her father had requested Logan's veterinary skills, especially with his opinion of Scottish men. "He must be concerned for his horses. Or was there another reason?" Cecily hoped the visit didn't have anything to do with their relationship.

Logan frowned. "I see your concern, but there's no need to worry. The visit had nothing to do with you and me. A horse has been acting strangely. I suspect he's too concerned about the situation to pay much attention to us."

"I'm relieved to hear it." Cecily sighed, then leaned closer to Logan, whispering: "Father cares about his horses, but he doesn't usually talk to those lower than him."

Logan shrugged, giving her the eye. "Lass, he talked to me." Cecily stared at him dreamily. Who wouldn't talk to Logan?

"I'm surprised you were asked to administer care, that's all. Was a horse unwell, or did he ask you to Carleton House under false pretenses?"

"If you're implying the visit had something to do with us, you couldn't be more wrong. One of the mares has been acting up. Your father's concerned about her. You know, maybe his horses can help him put aside his feelings for those lower than him."

"You're not less of a man, but that would be great if it were possible."

"Anything's possible," Logan said, pointing at himself. "How could he not take a liking to me? Have you not heard the gossip? I'm an animal whisperer." Logan leaned closer to her, smiling. "I have a talent in human relationships, too."

He looked at her in such a way that she almost melted under his heady perusal. Logan certainly had a lovability that drew her closer to him. He could whisper in her ear anytime he wanted.

"I'm not saying that changing my father's opinion is a foregone conclusion, but it would be great if it were possible." Cecily lowered her voice. "It would make our courtship easier as well."

"I'll be dropping by a bit later. Would you have time for a visit?"

"Oh…" Cecily welcomed the opportunity. She loved spending time with Logan.

"Maybe we can sneak in something more personal."

"What, another kiss?" Cecily pursed her lips. A kiss would suit her fine.

"If you're willing." Ah…just the thought of it caused her cheeks to heat and by the look on Logan's face, he welcomed the idea as much as her.

Ruth tapped her baton on a wooden stand, calling the choir to attention. "I have some announcements prior to starting. We're one week away from the Christmas Eve service, and unfortunately, Emmaline and Oliver can no longer sing."

"Are they ill?" Cecily asked.

"A throat infection apparently. Logan and Cecily, I was hoping you could take their place and sing the duet."

Logan's eyes widened. He seemed terrified. "I can't possibly. I've only just joined the choir. Singing in the company of these fine singers is one thing," he said, gesturing to the other members, "but getting in front of the entire congregation? Letting them hear my voice? What if I make a mistake? They'll laugh at me. I can't do it."

Cecily giggled. "You're not shy, Mr. Campbell. Furthermore, if I can do it, you can do it."

Logan's eyes rose. "Do you want to sing with me?"

Cecily wanted him to do a whole lot more than sing with her, and judging by the twinkle in his eye, he'd be interested in the pursuit. "Nothing would give me more pleasure."

"I'll do it, but I can't promise that I'll do a respectable job." Logan winked at her.

Ruth tapped the stand a second time. "You'll need to practice every day until Christmas Eve. Do you think you can manage the time?"

Cecily thought about the extra time she'd be in Logan's company. The thought of seeing him more often, hugging him, kissing him, filled her with joy. Maybe the sick horse could work to their advantage.

"You know, I'm always on call in case an animal needs attention. I can't promise that we'll be able to practice every day."

"Do your best."

Cecily nudged his foot with her own, smiling. She couldn't wait for the week ahead. She thanked whatever good fortune that had made it possible for her and Logan to spend more time together. A little lady luck and a couple's illness, too.

"What will we sing?" Logan asked.

"O Holy Night," Cecily replied. She touched his knee.

"Don't worry. Don't look so frightened. I'll be right beside you. You'll sound amazing."

*You are amazing...*Joy of joys, his sweet voice, his ginger hair and hazel eyes, everything about Logan Campbell compelled further investigation.

CHAPTER FOURTEEN

"*E*asy, girl…"

Logan administered care to Lady Luck. He fingered the space between the horse's withers and her lower neck, the intramuscular bulk between the two areas. He pinched skin coated with coarse hair and gently inserted the needle. Lady Luck jerked momentarily, just once. "You're okay, girl." He pulled on the plunger, ensuring no blood drew into the syringe; only then did he administer the vaccine.

Once the horse was vaccinated, he massaged the area. "You did well, Lady Luck."

Logan pulled out the needle, recapped it, and addressed the owner. "John, I brought an immune therapy with me. Like you, I have concerns. In case she's fighting an illness, giving her a supplemental treatment might be wise." Logan scratched his chin. "I don't understand what the underlying condition might be, but if it is rabies, the risk to Lady Luck could be great."

John leaned against the stall. "Tell me about the therapy."

"It requires four doses."

John studied him in a shrewd manner. He rubbed his chin. "Will it help?"

"Help her?" Logan studied the horse, its stretched neck, its dull eyes. He patted her neck. "The treatment could save her life. Especially if Lady Luck has an underlying illness, compromising her immune system. The immune globulin contains antibodies that fight infection. Even though her symptoms are minor, they're worrisome."

"How much does it cost? The vaccine's expensive."

"It's more expensive than the vaccine, but how much is your mare's life worth to you?" Logan gestured at the horse in the stall.

Logan studied John, watching him weigh the health and wealth subject. He scratched his head and exhaled in a breathy whisper, "Damn it."

Logan gave John a sympathetic look but didn't say anything, letting the owner make the decision.

"She's worth everything to me." John shook his head. He sighed. "I fell in love with her the first time I saw her. Just look at her...gorgeous chestnut color, white socks on her back legs, an impeccable pedigree. She's only four years old."

If John hadn't been describing his horse, Logan would have thought he was referring to his wife. The poor man spent too much time in the stable. "There's something more. Who foaled her?"

"That's a good observation. Nasturtium. Breeding costs

were out of this world, but the foal could earn me a windfall of money. You understand why I can't take any risks."

"I understand." The father of Lady Luck's foal didn't matter much to Logan. The health and welfare of all animals took precedence over someone else's idea of perfection.

"Give her the shots," John said.

Logan didn't tell John the immunization might not benefit the horse now that symptoms were present. He recognized the potential for a bad outcome so didn't disclose the entire truth. Such news would only add burden and John seemed worried enough. Though he was confident an immune shot was the right decision, to give the horse a fighting chance and her master hope. Hope was a key factor, especially during the Christmas season.

"You're making an excellent choice by lessening the risk. The globulin can't go in the same place as the vaccine. I'll need help administering it. Don't want her to bite me."

"I'll get Samuel," John replied. He left the stable.

HEELS CLICKED across the cobblestoned floor. Logan turned to see who it was. Cecily? "You shouldn't be here. It's not safe."

"I came to get a horse." She searched in the direction her father had gone. "I had to see you."

"Oh? Planning on taking a ride?"

"Yes," she said, staring at him coyly. "It's a pleasant afternoon. There's a trail alongside the lake. I like to ride beside it sometimes."

"I know the place." Logan moved closer to the railing. She was gorgeous standing this close. Her red bonnet and matching coat enhanced her appearance. He couldn't look away from her sparkling eyes and sweet pink lips that reminded him of rose petals in the summer. He wanted to kiss her. Taste her sweetness.

She shifted closer to the stall and touched its edge. He glanced at her gloved fingers. Too close to him. So close he could touch her hand. But as he was visiting her father's stable, he didn't dare.

"When you're finished with the horse," she said, whispering, "I thought we could meet." She smothered a laugh, stifling the sound. Was he her secret joy? She certainly was his.

He nodded. "Nothing would give me more pleasure. I'd meet you anywhere." He looked for John and Samuel. "I'll come as soon as my work is done. You better go before your father comes back."

"Don't take too long." She blew him a kiss. "I'll meet you at our place near the lake." He smiled, imagining their future home.

Logan watched Cecily as she moved toward a stall and collected a mare. The horse had excellent conformation, but he couldn't keep his eyes off Cecily. The petite coat tapered nicely to her waist and flared to her knees. She walked along the aisle, leading a horse, her hips swaying. His head filled with desire while considering other attributes. Full kissable lips, dark hair he'd like to brush his fingers through.

She was exiting the stable when her father returned with Samuel.

"Are you taking Fancy Foot for a ride?" John asked his daughter.

"It's a gorgeous day. Not too cold. The sunshine is brilliant and not a cloud in the sky. Thought I'd take a ride by the lake."

"Be on your way, then. Be careful."

"I will. Is Lady Luck better? I see Mr. Campbell is with her."

"She's about the same. But off you go. We have work to do."

AFTER CECILY LEFT THE BARN, John approached Logan, scratching his head. If he had concerns about the two of them, he didn't mention anything. At first, Logan thought Cecily's arrival in the stable had sparked John's curiosity, but Logan let the worry go when Samuel came into the stall and haltered Lady. They blindfolded her eyes as well, just in case. Then Samuel held the horse's head while he injected her in the pectoral muscle.

Logan was placing the syringe inside his doctor's bag when John asked him a pointed question. "Is there something going on between you and my daughter?"

Logan looked him in the eye. "Why do you ask?"

"I know my daughter. Something is off with her."

It appeared that John was an observant man and not only

with his horses. "She's probably told you we're singing in the choir together."

"Yes, she has. But I have this nagging feeling." John stared at him expectantly, waiting for a reply.

Logan wasn't the type to hide the truth or give an outright lie. Sometimes, a man had to fight for what he wanted. "I like Cecily well enough. I want to court your daughter."

John frowned. His face wrinkled with distrust. "What? Is she aware of your intentions?"

"This might surprise you, but Cecily has feelings for me, too."

John shook his head. "The nerve of you. I knew it. You'll stand aside and back off. You're not right for my daughter."

Logan grasped his doctor's bag, opened the stall door and passed through it. "How would you know what's right for Cecily?"

"I'm her father."

Logan sniffed, closing the gate. "That doesn't give you the right to decide her future."

John's stance seemed predatory; his attitude warped, as if he'd fight to protect his own. Would the Englishman get aggressive with him? Logan didn't think so. John placed his hands on his hips. His right hand clenched into a fist.

"Who better to decide, you?" John asked. "A veterinary surgeon from a poor class of people, and besides that, you're a Scotsman."

Logan's brows rose. "Given you're the father of the lass I care for, I'll try not to take offense. However, this ground we're standing on isn't in England. There's no reason for us to face each other with narrow-mindedness. But even if we were living in our homeland, I'd still care for Cecily."

"You can't court her."

Logan harrumphed. "You can't stop me."

"You bastard," John said, taking a step toward him. "You're taking advantage of the situation. I need your help. There's no other veterinary surgeon who can administer care to my horse."

Logan sighed. In this, John was right. Maybe he'd made a mistake in admitting the truth. The last thing he wanted to do was offend John or create a situation that would harm his horse.

"John, I've chosen to be honest with you about my feelings for your daughter. While I don't understand your issue, maybe in time, once you have a chance to know the real me, maybe you'll like me better."

"I like you well enough. I can see that Lady Luck likes you, too, but that's not the point."

Logan wondered if he could reason with this man. For the sake of Cecily, he had to try. "I've never had too many problems with animals. They accept me well enough. Still, I don't want to see Cecily in an underhanded way, but I will if you force me to."

"I don't have a say in my own daughter's future?"

"Look, you select the studs for your mares, but you can't do the same for your daughter. Let her decide who she should love."

"Heart. Love— Such sentiments don't feed a family."

"I can provide for your daughter. It can't hurt having a

son-in-law who can help with your horses. Would certainly assist with the vet expenses. Family get better rates."

"Is that so? I thought you were an animal whisperer, but I see Cecily is no more than a money-making opportunity to enter a wealthy family."

Logan shook his head. "No...nothing like that. I earn a good income from my veterinary services. I can provide for your daughter. Though, I've always been open to bartering, so I don't always bring home a coin. But a loaf of bread as payment for my services is adequate if it helps an animal."

John placed his hands on his hips. "I should throw you out of here, but I appreciate your honesty."

"Take some time to get to know me. Maybe you'll change your mind."

"I doubt it."

"There's one more thing," Logan said, appealing to John, "Cecily and I will be singing a duet at the Christmas Eve service. It's a sudden change in the program and we need a place to practice."

"The plot thickens."

"John, give me a chance. I tell you what. Let me practice with Cecily, in your home, under your watchful eye or Mrs. Carleton's. I'll help you with the vaccine and immune treatment expense."

"You're what, bribing me now, bartering with me like the other neighbors?"

"I care for your daughter," Logan said, his tone laden with melancholy. "I'd like to be on good terms with her parents."

"All right," John said, sighing. "I'll lose this fight anyway.

Just so you know, I'm not agreeing to anything more than two people practicing music. For the church's sake. I can't have God or the community coming down on me because they're lacking two soloists for the Christmas Eve service."

"Thank you, John."

"I suppose you're meeting her soon."

"I'll be the perfect gentleman. I'll be on my best behavior."

John sighed again. Then pointed his finger at him. "If you hurt her, I'll break your arm. If you compromise her…"

Logan passed by John. "None of that. I respect your daughter. And you as well."

He'd be the perfect gentleman, even though he wanted to smother Cecily with kisses and satisfy his deepest longings.

"I'll hold you to the promise to ease my expenses."

Logan nodded. "I'll return tomorrow to practice with Cecily. The day after I'll vaccinate Lady Luck again."

"Will you give her a second immune treatment as well?"

"Yes, I will."

John stood beneath him as he mounted his draft horse in the yard. "I'm not happy about you seeing my daughter, but I'm grateful for your care. You might not be right for Cecily, but the neighbors were right, you're a good horse doctor."

Logan offered a half-smile, wondering why John had praised him. "Give me a chance to change your opinion." He urged the horse forward, but then paused. "You need joy in your heart, John Carleton. Maybe Cecily and I can give you some. Why don't you attend the practice tomorrow?"

"Maybe I will."

Logan nudged his draft horse in the side and left John, making his way to the place by the lake. He felt good about having told John the truth about his feelings for Cecily. John wasn't partial to him, but time had a way of changing a man's viewpoint.

CHAPTER FIFTEEN

ecily's breath caught in her throat at the sight of Logan even before he reined in alongside her. Astride her own horse, she studied his hazel eyes and rosy cheeks. The ginger hair that dusted his shoulders. The woolen coat that added a snug weight to his girth. She smiled enthusiastically, overjoyed to see him. A part of her still couldn't believe she was in a relationship with this man, Logan Campbell.

"What are you up to, Cecily?" Logan asked. "You're staring at me as if you're plotting mischief. I should be back at your father's stable, minding a horse, rather than chasing you across the countryside."

She felt guilty for taking him away from Lady Luck, but only slightly. She had plans of her own, but matters of the heart were not as important as a sick horse. "I'm not sure what you're suggesting. A lady doesn't lower herself to mundane plots." Her voice came off cheeky. Logan's brows rose.

"Really? If I didn't know you better, I'd think you were lying. It's not like you to lie." He gave his horse a slight nudge, urging it closer to her, but Logan was right to be suspicious. She had carefully planned a private meeting at a secluded location. The excitement coursed through her veins, causing her cheeks to pinken.

Logan's expression widened into a half-smile. "I didn't think we'd see each other today."

Cecily's horse shifted beneath her. "Didn't you? We have a song to sing. I thought we should practice before the sun goes down."

He glanced at the horizon. "Is that the truth of it, or is there some other reason you want me to ride with you?"

"Of course, I wanted to share more time with you." To kiss him again…to feel his arms wrapped around her.

"We don't have much time. I have to have you home before it gets dark or your father will hunt me down like a fox on the run."

Cecily was too excited to pay much attention to the warning, and her father wasn't a concern, not with a sick horse. "There's a hunter's cabin not far from here. We need a place to practice. I thought we could go there."

"Ah, so you were scheming," Logan said, peering at her in a laid-back way. "This is a bad idea. Lass, if your father finds out the two of us have been sharing private moments at his cabin, you'll put me in a heap of trouble."

In that moment, getting caught didn't worry her. Practicing a song didn't concern her either. Cecily wanted to be alone with Logan. "I'll never tell him." She urged her mare into a canter, galloping in the cabin's direction. Logan followed closely behind. She glanced at him, giving him a haughty look, her eyes expressing her wants and needs. "You won't tell him either."

Logan's eyes lit with interest. "Who am I to prevent a lady's methods."

When he gave her a wolfish grin, Cecily did question if she was making the right decision, but her heart's desire spurred her onward. A lady shouldn't be without her suitor.

LOGAN PURSUED CECILY through the snow like a puppy trailing its owner, thinking the entire time that spending time with Cecily—alone in a private cabin—was a bad idea. Especially since he'd given up the secret that he cared for her to her father. What a mistake. Could he not have waited?

Cecily rode near him. When she turned her head, gauging if he'd come after her, he couldn't avoid her beauty. Her sweet face, her eyes glossed over with need, her cheeks flushed pink. The coldness of the season might have teased the color into her expression, but he suspected not. Her grin, more so than the lick across her lips, almost undid him.

Cecily expressed a desirous plea, and in response, his gut wrenched with need, his groin throbbing with intent to satisfy that need. "Cecily," he groaned. *What are you doing?*

She galloped faster. He pursued her.

He nudged his draft horse in the flanks, and it easily caught up.

Logan swallowed, forcing his desire to obey a weakening will. "Maybe we should turn back for home," he called out. "The sun, you see, it's falling. We shouldn't ride after dark."

Cecily scoffed at his warning. "Maybe we should ride faster, if only to reach the cabin sooner," she said, giving him a scandalous smirk prior to spurring her horse onward. It set off. Logan listened to her trill of laughter and the horse's hooves pounding against the ground. He nudged his horse and gave chase, following in her wake.

When they reached the cabin, he vaulted from his draft horse and hurried to Cecily's side, assisting her to dismount. He grasped her tiny waist, and she gripped his shoulders, slowly easing alongside him. She paused then, staring into his eyes, and then grasped his hand without saying a word and escorted him inside the cabin.

That look in her eyes. The need he saw there. He couldn't satisfy it. Not until they were man and wife.

As soon as the door shut, she edged him against the wood and kissed him.

"Cecily..."

"I've been dying to kiss you since our first kiss. Can we hold each other? Can I touch you?"

Oh aye—Logan wanted Cecily to touch him and more besides, but physical intimacy would break a promise he'd made to John Carleton. He reached for her and she nestled in his arms, their lips touching...so close he could smell her breath and the sweet scent of violet perfume. Grasping her waist, he traced the small of her back with his fingers.

Cecily moaned.

He removed his glove and stroked her cheek, seeing the naked regard in her eyes. "Lass, it would be safer to sing."

"There's lots of time for music."

"The night is falling fast and the Christmas Eve service is only days away. I don't even…"

Cecily kissed away his concern. "Why the worry? I want to kiss you. I need to hold you. I…"

Logan suspected she desired much more than he could give, and he wouldn't compromise her. He'd made a promise to her father. They couldn't do anything more than hug and kiss until Cecily Carleton was his wife. But he would satisfy her emotions. He kissed her lips, tasting her sweetness, then strove for his own patience while tucking her head beneath his chin.

Logan sang: "O holy night—my heart is too fast beating. This is the night I proclaim my love for you."

Cecily giggled, leaning against his chest. "Those are not the right lyrics, but I appreciate them all the same."

He laughed. "I hardly know the words."

"Let me teach you." Cecily laughed, her hands wandered into his coat and up to his shoulders. "Long did I wait, for you to come and find me, now that you're here, I feel complete."

"That doesn't sound right either, but I like what you're saying." Logan sang, "a thrill of joy, my weary heart rejoices…"

"…for yonder moon, lights a new and marvelous day."

Logan bent to his knees. "I fall…on my knees."

Cecily did the same, clutching his hand. "I hear…love in the making."

Logan and Cecily said together, "Oh night, divine. Oh, night…"

Logan stopped singing, realizing he was on his knees. He clutched Cecily's hands close to his heart. A look of wonder brightened her eyes. "Cecily, I want to marry you. I want to have you as my wife."

She sighed, staring at him. "I want you as my husband. Are you asking me?"

"I want to. I can't. Not yet."

"If you want to ask me for my hand in marriage, why don't you?"

"Lass, I require your father's blessing."

She frowned. His heart skipped a beat. Logan wished he'd never voiced the sentiment.

"He'll never give it," Cecily said with a sigh.

Logan pulled her into his embrace and kissed her forehead. "He'll agree. I'll help him understand." He'd already begun to help a father understand that he couldn't hold onto his daughter forever. Logan just needed a little lady luck. He wasn't known for human whispering.

"I love you, Logan."

No one had *ever* whispered sweeter words to him. "I love you too, sweet Cecily."

CHAPTER SIXTEEN

apa was late for dinner. Mother hadn't wanted to hold back the meal, so she'd instructed the housekeeper to serve it without the master of the house. They had already eaten soup and sweet breads. Cecily was savoring a bite of pheasant, recalling special moments with Logan, when her father entered the dining room.

"I apologize for my tardiness," John said, seating himself. "My lateness couldn't be helped."

Lillian gave her husband an impertinent stare. "The horses take precedence over everything. It's a wonder you don't eat in the stable."

Father made a face. Cecily cringed, fearing his wrath, but she knew a horse was ill. "Lillian, you have the horses to thank for this meal. Nothing comes into this house or onto this table without my labor. I get little thanks for the effort."

Cecily was accustomed to her mother's grumbling and her father's indifference, but he seemed more upset than usual.

Maybe the conversation should be taken in a less aggressive direction. "We understand, Papa. Don't we?"

Did it matter that her father was late? Cecily gave her mother an earnest look, appealing for calm. Lillian didn't say another word, choosing to focus on her meal. She quietly stabbed at carrots on her dinner plate while giving her daughter a pitiful look. The quiet posturing that dwelled in this room, almost every night, frustrated Cecily. What could she do to calm the tension? "I heard a horse was unwell, Papa. Mr. Campbell told me as much at choir practice."

Father's expression didn't alter, and perhaps became worse. "Mr. Campbell?" Father gave her a pinching stare.

"Yes, Father. Logan Campbell. He's joined the choir. It surprises me he has time to sing with all the animals that need his attention. Apparently, including our own."

John sighed. "Logan did stop by, for all the good it did. The horse is still unwell."

"I'm surprised you trusted Logan to examine the horse, given your feelings for him."

"Cecily, I'm not in the mood for confrontation this evening. This has been a troubling day."

Cecily took a bite of her meat and nibbled. "Papa, is the horse deathly ill? I've never seen you so upset."

He clutched his wine glass. "It doesn't appear so," Father said, running his fingers through what remained of his hair. A somber look clouded his eyes as if he had returned to the stable. "Though something's not right. I can't understand why the horse is acting strangely, but there is hope as well."

"Did Logan's consideration help?" Oops, she'd said his first name.

If her father noticed, he didn't draw attention to the mistake. "He did more than help. He dropped off a load of root vegetables and gave Lady Luck a vaccine. The weather, the diet, even illness could be a factor. Even so, something still doesn't feel right."

"Should Logan return?" Cecily certainly wanted him to return.

"He's stopping by tomorrow. Says the two of you have a duet to practice." Father's eyebrows rose curiously.

The statement surprised Cecily. "Oh, so you know. Oliver and Emmaline are ill. They cannot sing." Cecily made the mistake of a slight smile. "Logan is horrified. Not only to sing, but he doesn't know all the words. Who knows what will come out of his mouth." Father frowned.

"I'll permit it for the sake of the Christmas Eve service, but only if you practice in the drawing room." He glanced at her mother. "You must be chaperoned."

Cecily was shocked beyond words. One week her father was upset that a Scottish man drove his daughter home, and the next he allowed her to sing with him? Why?

"I'm grateful and surprised. Why are you agreeing to this?"

John tapped his fingers on the table. He sipped his wine. "There's no other veterinary surgeon in Essex now that William has returned to England. I'm worried about Lady Luck. Logan can check on her after the practice."

Cecily let the discussion drop. Father's attention was

completely on his horse, and she didn't want to upset him with nuggets of information that could challenge her emerging relationship.

Abigail piped up. "Christmas is coming. Papa, when will the search for the tree begin?"

He munched on his pheasant, contemplating. "I won't have time to manage a tree hunt this year. I'm sorry, Abigail. We may not have a tree."

Abigail visibly saddened. Cecily glanced at her mother, hoping she'd intercede, but she imparted the same worn-out message. "The horses always take precedence. Over everything. You probably won't have time for Christmas dinner."

"Depends on the horse and her health." Father stared at her mother. "I invested heavily in this horse. She carries an important foal."

"Mama, could you be more understanding?" Cecily asked. "Can't you see Papa's upset?"

"Papa," Abigail interjected, "why couldn't Cecily and I manage the search? We could address the issue with the staff? The tree should be dealt with. We can see you have worries of your own."

"How would you manage it?"

Cecily squeezed her fork. "Abigail wants a tree on the Campbell land. We passed by it the day we helped Granny with the Christmas pudding."

"No. It's not possible. Making such a request would give the wrong impression to the eldest son." Father stared at her in a curious way.

"How so?" Cecily asked. "It's just a tree."

John frowned, clearly averse to the idea. "I don't want Logan getting the wrong idea."

"About what?"

"About you. It's enough I agreed to let you sing together."

"I can't believe you agreed to it."

"Well, I can't have God or the community angry with me because I didn't permit: *O Holy Night*."

"Yes, of course, but Mrs. Campbell has been ill. And your horse is ill. Papa, if it's okay with you, I'd like to take Mrs. Campbell a goodwill basket. Maybe some bread. I'd ask about the tree, of course."

"And I'd go as well. To chaperone Cecily." Abigail gave their father a pleading look. "Please, Papa, can we go?"

Father scratched his head. "It must be an amazing tree."

"It's a fine tree," Cecily said. The tree was perfect in every way but visiting the Campbell family gave her another opportunity to see Logan.

"I can't believe I'm agreeing to this," Father said. "All right, do it. Take a basket, some preserves and bread for the family. And Cecily…"

"…yes, Papa?"

"Go at first light tomorrow morning. Ask Logan to return. Tell him Lady Luck's health is getting worse."

Cecily perused her father's expression. Melancholy cast his eyesight downward. A depressed mien that told her more than words ever could that his horse could die. That look squeezed at her heartstrings. Why was she being selfish?

Desiring an opportunity to see Logan again when a sick horse needed his attention?

"Will the horse be okay overnight? Should someone request Logan's medical assistance sooner?"

"No. Samuel's watching the horse over night."

The dinner hour continued, but Cecily worried about the horse and its care. Sometimes she felt helpless as a woman. She should be in the stable, too.

CHAPTER SEVENTEEN

It wasn't usual for family members to go below stairs to address a personal request, but Cecily wanted to thank the staff for their assistance. She strode down the stairway and into the corridor, smelling the aroma of freshly baked bread.

The staff were busy. Christmas was coming closer and with it a daily flurry of activity. When Cecily entered the kitchen, Alice, the cook, stood near the worktable, stirring flour and spices in a bowl, while Nettie, her assistant, scrubbed various gadgets at the washstand. The basket was ready and sitting on the receiving table.

"Good morning, Lady Cecily," Alice said, pausing from her work. She washed her hands and dried them on a towel.

"A good day to you as well," Cecily replied, imparting a smile. "I've come to collect the gift basket for the Campbell family."

"It's ready." Alice gestured toward the basket. "It's

generous of you to give the Campbell family such a gift. They'll appreciate Mr. Carleton's kindness."

"If the bread tastes as good as it smells, they'll be more grateful to the cooks. The family will appreciate your food preparation. After all, I didn't prepare the food."

"From what I've heard, you supplied the means for it to happen."

"I don't deny it," Cecily said, "but I appreciate your hard word and thank you for it, especially since the request came with little notice."

Alice waved the concern away. "It's no bother. Would you like to see the contents?"

"Yes, I would. Please."

Alice moved nearer to the basket. As Cecily stepped closer, she saw the cook had layered the insides of the basket with tea towels. The attention to detail impressed her.

"We bake bread on Mondays, so I've included a couple loaves, fresh scones, blackberry jam, clotted cream and cheese. With Christmas drawing nearer, I thought a pint of mincemeat would complement the gift."

"You've thought of everything. Thank you."

Nettie piped up. "We haven't prepared much of the Christmas baking yet, but fortunately for the Campbell children, Alice and I prepared candy canes last week. There's a couple handfuls in the basket."

"Yes, I see them. The Campbell children will appreciate this more so than the bread, especially so since sugar is a luxury item. It's not every day a child receives a sweet treat."

Esther Mason, the housekeeper, came into the kitchen just

then. "Bad for the teeth if you ask me." She placed her hands on her hips. "Good morning, Lady Cecily."

"A good day to you as well, Esther."

"Have you come to fetch the basket? It's ready. We don't want to keep you from your journey." She peered at Alice. "Will you be using the cutter? Shall I ask Albert to assist you with the basket?"

"I'd appreciate his help. I'll be taking the sleigh."

"I'll have Albert instruct Samuel to have it prepared and brought round to the front of the house. Readied for your travel."

"Thank you, Esther."

Cecily suspected Alice had filled the basket with more items than had been divulged, and she was grateful. With Mrs. Campbell's health situation, the entire selection made a lovely gift.

When she arrived at the sleigh, Albert had placed the basket inside. Cecily climbed up to the driver's seat and grasped the reins. Abigail joined her and they set off to the Campbell farm.

"Are you excited to see Logan?" Abigail asked.

Cecily pulled on the reins, managing Cisco. "Yes, I am. I can't wait to see him again, though he might not be at the house, given his veterinary responsibilities."

Abigail gave her a knowing look. "I suppose we have a sick horse to thank."

"Lady Luck must be in terrible shape."

"Papa seemed worried. It's unusual he'd permit Logan to administer care to one of his horses."

Cecily knew what her sister was suggesting, but their father would never see an animal suffer. "Papa might be difficult at times, but he's an intelligent man. His horses are more than a means of wealth, which is why he spends so much time in the stable."

"More time with the horses than with our mother."

"If you ask me," Cecily said, "he loves his animals more than our mother."

"Explains why he only has two daughters."

"Let's not get into that subject." Cecily shook her head. "The point I'm trying to make is that Father wouldn't put his horses at risk."

"He must have returned to the barn after the evening meal. I heard him come in late last night. Must have been early in the morning."

Cecily flipped the reins, encouraging Cisco to quicken the pace. "Makes me feel guilty for having an ulterior motive in seeing Logan. Even more reason to make haste."

Cecily flipped the reins, guiding Cisco into a trot.

WHEN THEY REACHED the Campbell homestead. Cecily reined in Cisco, urging the horse to stop. She shifted the brake into place and then climbed down from the cutter.

"Should I get the basket?" Abigail asked.

Cecily met her sister on the passenger side of the sleigh. "It's heavy. We'll both need to carry it. You hold one handle; I'll hold the other."

They retrieved the basket from the sleigh and then approached the front entrance. Cecily knocked on the door. "What did Alice put in this basket?" Abigail made a face. "It's heavy."

"Happiness." Cecily said, smiling.

Mrs. Campbell opened the door. "Lady Cecily, Lady Abigail, this is a pleasant surprise." She glanced at the basket. "What brings you by today?"

"We've brought a gift for your family. Our father wanted to thank Logan for assisting him with one of his horses."

Mrs. Campbell swung the door open more fully. "That's kind of Mr. Carleton. I'm grateful to receive this blessing. Please, come inside."

They entered the Campbell home. The great room was quieter than the previous visit. A fire burned in the hearth. A patterned quilt lay on the sofa. Much different than the confusion Cecily had witnessed the night the choir had sung for the family. Now, everything was neatly in its place. "The children must be at school," Cecily said.

"All except Isla. Logan kindly gave me a break today."

"Another animal in need of care?"

Mrs. Campbell glanced at the basket. "I expect they'll be back soon. But tell me, what's inside the basket?"

With Abigail's help, Cecily placed the basket on the table. "Fresh bread, some preserves, candy canes for the children."

"You're too kind. Thank you for your generosity. I'll save

the candy canes for Christmas Day. They're sure to put a smile on the children's faces." Probably more energy-inducing activity around the manor house as well, but Cecily didn't voice this thought.

"Tell the children St. Nick brought them," Abigail added.

"I think not. They'll expect the merry man to come this way again next year and the year thereafter as well. No… I'll tell them the truth. It's best."

"Are you feeling better?" Cecily asked, stepping away from the table.

"Yes, I've been able to resume my daily chores, though I haven't felt like baking." Mrs. Campbell placed her hand on her belly. "Some smells still make me nauseous."

"I'm glad you're feeling better."

The door opened and Logan and Isla came inside the house. Cecily's expression brightened at the sight of him.

"What do we have here?" Logan asked, smiling. "This is a surprise."

"Hopefully a nice one," Abigail said, glancing at her sister. "We brought a gift for your family."

"You did?" Logan perused Cecily in an evocative way that could have suggested she was the gift. He removed his boots. He walked over to the basket and fingered the contents. "From what I can see, it's a generous gift."

Logan took hold of the crock and was about to remove the lid. "Put that down," Mrs. Campbell said, taking the crock from his hands.

Logan gave his mother a disappointed look. "I only wanted to look inside."

"And you will, on Christmas Day."

Logan looked at Cecily. "This is a generous gift. What did we do to earn such a bounty?"

"Father appreciated your recent help. He wanted to thank you for administering care to Lady Luck."

Logan made a face. Isla wandered over to their mother. "Oh? How is the horse?"

"I'm afraid she's still unwell," Cecily said, frowning. "In fact, Father would like you to take a second look. He fears the horse's health is worsening."

"I'm sorry to hear it. I was hoping she'd be better by now. Is there something more?" Logan asked.

"Actually, yes. Given the horse's health, Father won't have time to manage a search for our Christmas tree. Abigail and I were wondering if…"

Logan's eyes lit up. "Do you need help? Are you asking for mine?"

"In a word, yes."

Cecily beamed with joy. She couldn't help expressing her happiness at the thought of spending more time with the gentleman she secretly courted. Thanks to her sister, the tree gave her another opportunity to be with him.

"I'd love to help you out," Logan said.

"I wouldn't object if you found our tree," Mrs. Campbell interjected. "Christmas Eve is less than a week away and your father has been freighting on the lake. It's not Christmas without a tree."

"I can do that for you, Mother, but the health of the horse should come first. Before anything else. Shall I see to Lady

Luck? Maybe we search for the tree tomorrow?"

Abigail looked at Cecily in a hopeful way. "Actually, we've seen the perfect tree."

"Oh, where is it?"

Cecily was embarrassed to make the confession, but she soldiered on. "It's on your land. Abigail saw the tree a couple weeks back."

Abigail bit at her lip, clearly afraid that Logan would give them an outright no.

"Really? Let's go see it." Logan said.

"I'd love to, but Papa will be anxious."

"If you passed by it the other day, you'll have to do the same on your way home." Logan returned to the front door and put his boots on. "I'll get my bag and my horse, then we'll be on our way."

"After we look at the tree, you might as well come to the house. In addition, we also need to practice our song."

A look passed between them. An attractive appeal that brightened Cecily's eyes and blossomed on her cheeks as she recalled the previous day in the cabin. "We best hurry."

Cecily and Abigail returned to the front door.

"Please thank Mr. Carleton for the basket," Mrs. Campbell said. "Your gift will add joy come dinnertime."

"Our pleasure, Mrs. Campbell."

After saying their goodbyes, they left the manor house. Cecily and Abigail climbed into the cutter while Logan retrieved his horse. He drew alongside the sleigh, and they set off to look at the Campbell tree. Cecily didn't think she'd ever seen her sister so excited, but as they passed along the laneway and dashed across fields of snow, it wasn't a tree that drew her attention. Pleasant thoughts consumed her mind with Logan riding near the sleigh.

Cecily urged Cisco to a stop and applied the brake when they arrived at the Campbell tree. She and Abigail remained in the cutter, not knowing how deep the snow might be. Logan jumped from his horse and stood near the tree's trunk.

"I can see why you want it," Logan said, fingering the branches. "It's a beauty."

"True enough, but maybe it's thoughtless to ask for it, especially since your family needs a tree as well. Logan, maybe you should take it."

Shocked by Cecily's comment, Abigail's forehead furrowed. Pouting, she bit at her lip.

"Don't worry, Abigail," Logan said, stemming her fears. "A fool could see how much you love this tree. Who am I to rob you of it? It's yours. I'll find another tree for the family. Heck, there's an entire forest of trees on this land." But as he voiced the sentiment, not once did he look at the forest. Logan studied Cecily in a sensual way that warmed her heart.

Abigail didn't notice the rapture happening between them and clapped her hands. "Thank you, Logan."

"Does this tree make you happy?" he asked, grinning.

"Tremendously," Cecily replied. "You're a good man, Logan."

"It's nothing. As far as I'm concerned, it's a stick of wood rooted in the ground. Wood to build a home," he said, winking, "or kindling to heat fireplace walls."

"Should the taking-down wait until tomorrow?"

Logan nodded. "Aye. I should see to the horse."

"Let's be off then."

They traveled to Carleton House in good spirits. Once they reached their destination, Logan left Cecily and Abigail near the front entrance.

CHAPTER EIGHTEEN

Logan heard angry snippets of conversation even before he passed through the pitching door and into the stable. He walked along the aisle, concerned about the situation. He saw Samuel speaking to John near Lady Luck's stall. His face was beet red, one hand clasped into a fist, but one look at the horse informed Logan the conversation related to its health.

"What's changed?" Logan asked. They hadn't realized he'd entered the stable. Both men stared at him in surprise.

Logan waited for John to reply. He looked terrible, like he hadn't slept in days. His eyes were bloodshot, his hair mussed, his clothing in disarray. He kicked at the floor before running a hand through his silver hair. "She's getting worse. It's happening right before my eyes, and it makes me feel so damn helpless. I don't know what to do. Samuel isn't making the situation any easier to accept."

Logan squeezed the handle of his vet bag. It looked like

he'd have to manage the humans, too. "Okay, let's try to stay calm. We're not helping the horse, or each other, by losing control. Tell me about her symptoms."

"She's stopped drinking. When touched, she gets snappy," Samuel replied.

"Okay, that's concerning, but not entirely surprising," Logan said, his tone soft and easy. "Is it safe to go inside the stall?"

"Maybe."

"Samuel, you're not reassuring me."

"She hasn't acted out. Not yet, but I'm worried she might."

Logan opened the stall door and went inside, preparing to check the horse's vitals. Lady Luck tolerated his presence, so he retrieved his thermometer then placed the bag on the ground. He took her temperature. "Her temperature is slightly elevated, but not terribly. Unless something changes, you don't need to concern yourself about it at this point."

"If it's not normal, why are you unconcerned?"

"Did I say I wasn't concerned?" Logan asked. "Look, she's had a vaccine. It's added a pathogen inside her body, which could be elevating her temperature." Logan didn't tell John that a raised temperature could also indicate illness, or infection, but by the way John was acting, he probably knew this already.

Logan grabbed his stethoscope and listened to Lady Luck's heart and lungs. "Her heart rate is elevated as well."

"What do we do?"

Logan placed his medical equipment back inside his bag.

"I'll give her another shot of immune globulin to help her fight."

"You think there's more to this. The look on your face confirms my worst fears. You can't hide it from me."

Logan raised his hand. "No one's hiding anything. My main concern arises from the fact she's stopped drinking."

John nodded, placing his hands on his hips. "That concerns me, too."

"Look, John, all we can do is watch her. If this is an illness, she has to fight it."

"What if it's rabies?"

"I hope not, but you must prepare yourself for the worst. If your horse has rabies, there's little anyone can do."

Logan scrutinized Lady Luck, worrying. She was a beautiful animal. Such a crime if this horse carried a deadly virus. But he wouldn't give up. Not yet.

John nodded. He took a deep breath. "Will you do everything possible?"

Logan felt helpless. "Yes, of course." He gave Lady Luck another shot of immune globulin, then retrieved his bag and exited the stall.

"What about the water situation?" Samuel asked.

"Try adding salt to the hay or soaking the hay in water. Did you give her boiled turnips last night?"

"Yes."

"Great. Keep doing that," Logan said. "I hate to leave you, but I need to practice for the Christmas Eve service. Is that okay? Or do you want me to stay with Lady Luck?"

"Shit." John shook his head. "No. You've done all you can here. You go, see to the practice."

Logan passed by John. "I'll check on Lady Luck again this afternoon."

"Thank you," John replied.

Logan felt guilty for leaving the situation. He worried the horse's condition would get worse.

CHAPTER NINETEEN

Cecily lounged in the drawing room while waiting for Logan. The staff were decorating the Carleton home: gold ribbon tie bows adorned the cream staircase, floral wreaths festooned with balsam fir hung on either side of the fireplace. Even now, Esther directed servants on where to place several snippets of greenery. All that was left to do, in Cecily's opinion, was the central masterpiece—the Christmas tree.

When would Logan bring it?

She rose a little higher when a knock sounded at the door. Alfred answered the call and Cecily listened to brief introductions being made. Soon after, Alfred entered the drawing room. "Mr. Campbell to see you, Lady Cecily."

She smiled. "Show him in, Alfred. If you will, please let my mother and sister know that Mr. Campbell has arrived."

"As you wish."

When Logan entered the drawing room, Cecily rose from

her chair. "Welcome to Carleton House. I'd give you a hug," she whispered, giving him a knowing look, "but we'd be found out. There's more activity than usual in the house today. Too many curious people to catch us unaware."

"Best to mind our behavior then and avoid trouble." He gave her a wink, but she saw by the twinkle in his eye that he wanted the hug, maybe a kiss as well, as much as she.

He studied the room, observing the decorations. "Look at this beautiful home. The staff have been busy."

Cecily grasped his elbow and led him nearer to the grand piano. "They've been decorating all morning. Did you see the gold ribbons on the staircase?"

"One couldn't miss them."

Cecily frowned, peering at his hazel eyes. "Do you think it's too much?"

"No, of course not. I'd expect no less from the Carleton family. The floral wreath on the outer door certainly made an impression."

"I hope it gave off the right feel. Tidings of joy?"

Cecily saw his slight frown and wondered what it meant. "Abigail has been helping with the decorating. She loves this season more than any other."

Cecily knew Abigail had absconded with the mistletoe. That glimmer in her eye could only mean she intended to cause mischief of some sort. Where had she placed it?

Logan took a deep breath. "Smells amazing in here."

"It's the balsam fir. There's nothing like that scent to remind one of Christmas. Brings the trees inside."

Logan fingered a branch lying on the piano. "Aye, reminds me… I promised to get your tree. I won't let you down."

"You better not. Abigail would be devastated."

"We don't want that," Logan said, winking. "Are you ready to practice?"

"We'll begin shortly, as soon as our audience arrives," she said, lowering her voice. "Mother will chaperone, and Abigail will accompany us on the piano."

He tapped her nose. "I don't mind at all, but they'll be disappointed when they discover I don't know the words."

"Logan, are you nervous?"

"I'll make mistakes, no different than before."

"That's okay by me," Cecily said with a giggle, "your first interpretation of the song gave me more than I expected, but we should avoid a repeat performance for the sake of my mother and the congregation." She retrieved a piece of paper from her dress pocket and opened it. "I wrote the lyrics to rouse your memory. You can take them home after the practice."

Logan laughed. "Rouse my memory, hey. I thought the lyrics were in excellent form."

"Words to warm a lady's heart," Cecily said, giving him a simpering look while recalling their singing in the hunter's cabin. Logan's inspirational lyrics had filled her head with romance and love. Desire as well if she were honest about her emotions. How many men sang to a woman in such a way?

Be still my beating heart.

"My mother insists on observing the practice, apparently at Father's request."

"If I'm to practice in front of anyone, it might as well be family." He smiled, but his happiness faded away, his face wrinkling with concern.

Poor Logan. Cecily appreciated his willingness to practice in front of her family, yet *her* family didn't comfort Logan. He seemed nervous.

Lady Carleton and Abigail came into the room. "Mama, I don't think you've met Logan Campbell," Cecily said. Nerves rose in her now, too.

"We've never met, though I have had the pleasure of hearing you sing before." Mother sat on a chair near the piano. She straightened her taffeta skirt, wearing a thoughtful expression. With no further preamble she said, "Shall we begin?"

Abigail took a seat at the piano and began to play, her fingers gliding over the ivory keys, capturing the chords, one after another, fingering the ivories for the song *O Holy Night*. Cecily nodded at her sister and then at Logan, and they began to sing.

A fit of nerves, anxiety filled Cecily's lungs more so than air to sing, or maybe her mother's presence caused the unease. Her voice stuttered, delivering a strangled sound. One needed good air to carry a tune. "Stop!" Cecily said. "We need to start over."

Logan gave her a worried look. "Why? Your voice sounded wonderful."

"It's the exact opposite, I'm afraid. I sang terribly."

Abigail gave them a look and then began the opening notes a second time. This time, it was Logan who stopped the pianist. "I'm having a tough time reading your paper. It's difficult to find the words in this scrawl."

Cecily pouted. "You don't like my handwriting?"

Lillian Carleton's eyebrows rose. "Stop the pretense. It's obvious you have feelings for each other."

Cecily's mouth slipped open while staring at her mother. Shock filled her. Embarrassment caused her face to flame. How did one reply to such a comment?

Abigail struck a discordant tone on the keyboard.

"You can deny it all you want, but the passion is there. If I can see it, others will, too. You need to harness the emotion inside yourselves to create magic on Christmas Eve. Focus on the passion and the words will come out beautifully. Abigail, on the count of three, start again."

Cecily swallowed, waiting, staring at her mother. What had she said? What had she instructed them to do? Mother tapped her fingers on the chair, counting out her rhythm. "One, two, three…"

Cecily stepped closer to Logan, shyly gazing into his eyes. Even though they had an audience, he grasped her fingers and they began to sing: "O holy night…the stars are brightly shining. It is the night of our dear Savior's birth."

"That's better," Lillian said, nodding. "Now continue."

"Long lay the world in sin and error pining…"

By the time they reached the highpoint of the song, each of them had forgotten that anyone was watching. Cecily didn't know that her father had entered the house and was standing near the archway. She gazed into Logan's eyes, singing of hope on a divine night. Then of a glorious new morn, a place where angels' voices delivered the news of a child in a manger. When their harmony concluded, the last note on the piano drifted away to silence. No one said a word.

Finally, Abigail clapped her hands.

Cecily glanced at her mother, nibbling at her bottom lip. "How did we do? Do we need more practice?"

Mother smiled. "I'm impressed. Though you must sing the carol again; your voices serenaded me like sweet sugar and cinnamon spice. Quite beautiful, actually."

Cecily's father walked into the drawing room, nodding. He didn't utter a word. Tears glistened in his eyes. Cecily released Logan's hand. "What's wrong, Papa?"

"Is Lady Luck worse?" Logan asked.

"The horse is no worse. About the same." He wiped at his eyes. "A fool of a man became emotional for a moment."

John Carleton sat on a chair near his wife. Cecily stared at her parents, wondering what they were thinking, feeling? What might they say next? She'd been holding Logan's hand. What impression had she given them about her relationship with Logan and how did her father feel about the handhold?

"I'd like to hear the carol again." His response astounded her.

"Shall we call in the staff?" Lillian asked. "And give the singers a larger audience?"

"A splendid idea," John replied. "Alfred, please have the staff join us."

When all the servants were assembled in the drawing room, Lillian took charge. "At the count of three," she said, giving her daughter a supportive look, "One, two, three…"

This time there were no less nerves, especially with ten plus people in the room. Cecily smiled, feeling hopeful. They didn't quite capture the emotion as before, but she thought they sang reasonably well. When they finished, their audience clapped.

"All this singing has *roused* my hunger. It must be time for Afternoon Tea?" Oh my, Cecily thought, had her father heard their prior conversation? She wasn't drawing attention to her and Logan by commenting.

"It's early for luncheon, but I'd welcome a spot of tea," Lillian replied. "Esther, can the kitchen staff manage sandwiches and small cakes at this hour? We have a guest."

"We'll give it a go, Lady Lillian."

"That decides it," John said, clapping his hands. "You'll join us. Won't you, Logan?"

Shock filled Cecily. Father said Logan's first name as if they were well acquainted. What was happening here?

"Who can say no to small cakes," Logan replied, giving Cecily a happy look.

THE CARLETON FAMILY took their normal seats at the dining room table. Logan sat near Cecily and opposite Abigail. Father sat at the head of the table and her mother near him. Cecily appreciated that her parents had welcomed Logan to join them for tea. She took this as a positive sign.

"Tea for you, sir?" the footman asked.

"Yes, please," John Carleton said.

Cecily watched as the footman poured tea into her father's cup.

"Cecily," John said, drumming his fingers on the table. "I don't mean to cause embarrassment, but a question has been raised, one which I've been considering carefully."

"You have us in a morbid state of curiosity," Lillian said, eyeing Father. "Will you get on with it."

Father frowned, glancing at her mother in an indifferent way, as if her opinion didn't matter. "Don't burden me. I'm deciding how best to approach the subject."

Cecily took a sip of her tea, assuming her father wanted to talk about the song. "Say what's on your mind, Papa. A straightforward approach seems best."

"All right. Cecily, Logan has requested my permission, your mother's as well if you must know, to court you."

Cecily choked, almost spitting her tea on the table. She placed her teacup on its saucer. It clattered as it touched the surface. She was certain her face heated a brilliant shade of pink. She glanced at Logan. "What did you do?"

He shrugged. "I'm not one to lie or conceal the truth. I thought it best your father knew of my intentions."

"Your intentions best start with your intended."

"I asked you. I know how you feel."

"Yes, but you could have told me you discussed the possibility with my parents."

John cleared his throat. "Logan acted appropriately, and more honestly than my own daughter. Let me tell you, a man shouldn't court one's daughter without speaking to her father."

Cecily frowned. She wished she lived in a society where women had more choice in such matters. The frustration filled her chest and hurt her mind. She grasped her teacup and took another sip while striving for patience. "How do you feel about this courtship question?" Cecily asked, glancing at her father in a hopeful way.

"At first, I thought the idea was preposterous, especially given Logan's lower class." John looked at Logan. "I mean no disrespect, sir."

"None taken."

"Have you changed your mind?" Cecily asked, nibbling at her lower lip.

"Not entirely, but I'll tell you this, even a father can change his opinion. This isn't England. This is a new world with new ideas, and I admit it, I have lessons to learn. Knowledge to embrace. I see Logan's ability with horses and other animals. This won't surprise my daughter, but he's somewhat of a horse whisperer."

"My reputation precedes me." Logan sipped his tea.

"Cecily Carleton, how do you feel about Logan Campbell?" John asked.

Cecily took a deep breath, preparing to expose her truth. "I like him well enough."

"Enough to court him?"

Cecily nodded, absolutely terrified how her father might react.

"I thought as much. After watching you sing, I've decided to give my consent."

Cecily was shocked. What had her father just acknowledged? "You've what?"

He clasped his hands in front of him. He smiled. "You may court your heart's desire. Who am I to prevent my daughter from seeing a good man."

"I don't know what to say. How did you come to this decision?"

"It's simple. Logan's a veterinary surgeon. An accomplished medical doctor. Just what I need to assist in the management of my horses."

"And I'd be happy to offer my services to the Carleton family, as long as I can still assist the community that has come to depend on me."

"Of course," John said. "I wouldn't want to compromise animal health."

"Thank you, Papa," Cecily said, feeling emotional. Feeling as if she might cry.

"You're welcome, daughter." He lifted his teacup, minding everyone at the table. "May your love for each other fill this house with happiness."

Mother smiled, touching Father's hand. "We give you our blessing. To your future together."

Logan glanced at Cecily then, giving her the sweetest look. He grasped her hand beneath the table and she smiled at him, grateful that they could pursue a relationship and celebrate it with their family.

They broke contact when the servants brought small cakes, scones, and clotted cream into the dining room. Cecily glanced at Logan, her face aglow, her eyes bright, while pondering their coming days. She stared at her father, not sure how she'd thank him for his support.

Abigail sat quietly, her hands primly in her lap. Was her sister happy with this news? Did she reflect on Ian? Cecily suspected the answer to this silent question was yes.

CHAPTER TWENTY

One day later, Lady Luck's health took a turn for the worse. Logan stood outside her stall, assessing her condition, while John and Samuel argued about the treatment options. One was potentially deadly. Logan couldn't think clearly with all the bickering.

"I know you don't want to hear this, but a country vet can't make a bit of difference in the health of this horse," Samuel said. "She's showing signs of serious illness. If it is rabies, we need to end the suffering."

"Not on your life," John snapped, an edge in his voice. He swept his hand across his forehead. "She's carrying Nasturtium's foal."

"She's carrying death to the other horses if they catch it."

Logan sighed. He raised his hand in appeal. "Your arguing isn't helping the horse. There's no question Lady Luck is sick. The signs are obvious, but rash decisions and upsetting conversations won't make this better."

Logan felt relieved when the bickering stopped. He focused on the horse, considering the symptoms. She had a fever, but the higher temperature could be explained. Fever was a natural response to infection. The spasms, possibly the body's attempt to bring the fever down. But one look at John, who was struggling to come to terms with the situation, made him wish he could do more.

"We must remain calm," Logan said, moving closer to the stall. "Arguing won't help Lady Luck. Give me time to assess the situation."

Samuel snorted. "There's nothing to evaluate. The horse is sick and growing sicker by the minute. Look at her, look at the spasms."

Logan scanned Samuel's expression instead. Mussed hair, bloodshot eyes, and a face marred with soot and worry. His reasoning was flawed. He wore the same clothing as the night before. Poor guy, he probably hadn't been to bed yet.

"Samuel, you're exhausted. You were probably up all night taking care of her. I'm here now. I've heard your thoughts on the matter. Maybe you should take a rest."

Lady Luck screamed, then tossed her head. Logan moved closer to the railing, observing her behavior as one would observe disaster happening before their eyes while feeling helpless to do anything other than the desperate means Samuel had suggested.

"What else changed overnight?" Logan asked.

"She doesn't want to be touched. Seems more agitated."

"That symptom in itself is not a reason for concern."

Logan pressed against the railing to get a better look. He

didn't have to touch the horse to know the fever had worsened. Her eyes were crazed. Foam leaked from her mouth. Beads of sweat clung to the coat and muscle aches that had been minor the day before were more pronounced.

"Holy hell…" he muttered, his full attention on the horse rather than John or Samuel. Silent, Logan stared at Lady Luck, feeling helpless. He'd done everything by the book, following his training to the letter. Was it enough?

Logan shook his head. Samuel had made a valuable point. Lady Luck's health had worsened, which caused him no end of worry. But had the time come to end the horse's life? Would he abandon hope? No way! He wasn't ready to make that call.

"This horse is fighting something," Samuel said.

"That's obvious," John barked. "Help me out here. What more can we do?"

Logan worried his initial hunch was right. "We need to exhaust every option before we consider something fatal. I need to give Lady Luck a second dose of vaccine. Another shot of immune globulin; medication to help her fight the infection."

"Infection?" John froze.

Logan faced him. "I'm certain we have a case of rabies here."

John's face paled, his eyes widened. "When you first talked about the possibility, I had hoped it wasn't true. I had hoped you were wrong."

Logan studied the agitated horse. "If there's one positive

to take from this situation, she's not presenting with neurological symptoms. Maybe I vaccinated her in time."

Logan noticed the bandage. "John, have you been hurt?"

He sighed. "She bit me."

This news concerned Logan. "When?"

"Last night."

"We need to address the injury. Right now. John…there's no cure for rabies and you have been in contact with a possible case."

"What do I do?"

"I have vaccine with me. You can call on the local doctor or trust me to vaccinate you."

John's attention shifted to his hand. "It hurts something terrible."

"I bet."

John gave him a pleading look. "Please…save the horse."

Logan studied the desperation in John's eyes and while reflecting on the obvious sickness in Lady Luck, bearing in mind her suffering, considering she likely had rabies. Had he vaccinated her in time?

How unfortunate for such a beautiful creature. But now the horse may have infected its owner. Saving John, likely. Saving the horse, Logan didn't know if it was possible. But there was no way he was robbing John of hope.

"I don't know, John. No one has a window on the future. Right now, I'm more concerned about you, but I promise, I'll do everything I can."

John sighed. He stared at the ground.

"I need to examine your hand. I know you care about this horse, but you come first. Do you understand?"

John nodded.

"After I've given you medical attention, I need to get more vaccine. I don't have enough for the horse and its master," Logan said. "I'd like to borrow one of your thoroughbreds. I came on a draft horse and she's trustworthy, but slow."

"Midnight Blue is best. He won't throw you." John addressed the stable master. "Samuel, saddle the horse, then get yourself to bed. Logan's right. We're no use to anyone if we don't get enough rest."

Samuel left them to conduct the instructions.

Logan gave John a serious look. "Now, let's take care of your hand."

Cecily paced near the front window, hoping Logan would visit the house after administering care to Lady Luck. How much longer would he be? How long would her father rob her of his attention? Given her father's earlier concerns, his stormy eyes, furrowed brow and brooding silence, the situation must be dire. Even so, when the door opened at the back of the house, she hurried toward it, excited to see who had entered the house.

Logan stood in the entranceway with her father. "Cecily, your father is hurt."

"Oh no, should I arrange for the doctor to come?" Cecily asked.

"Not yet. I'll examine the wound and clean it. Due to the circumstances, no one should touch it but me." He walked near her father. "John, where is the best place to treat you?"

"My bedchamber," John said, wincing. "Don't look so worried, Cecily. The horse hardly broke through the skin."

Cecily made a face, envisioning a massive jaw and a full set of teeth clamping down on her father's hand. She paused in the middle of the hallway, swaying, wondering…what should she do?

"Let's get you to your bedchamber," Logan said, ushering her father toward the staircase. "Cecily, call for the butler. Have him meet us in your father's room. I'll need a bowl, clean cloths, and hot water."

"All right."

Cecily glanced at the bandaged hand, watching them climb the stairs to the upper floor.

"Cecily…" Logan said, appealing to her in a calm manner. "Your father's okay. I need your help."

"Of course," she said, taking a deep breath, rallying for self-control.

Cecily normally rang the bell to call on the servants, but this practice wouldn't be quick enough. She rushed to the servants' work area, entering a busy kitchen.

Esther noticed her first. "Is something wrong, Lady Cecily?"

"Father's been hurt." Her heart pounded, her breathing too loud and too fast. "Logan has requested Alfred's help. He needs a basin, warm water, and clean cloths." Cecily fought for calm.

"Where is Mr. Carleton?"

"In his bedchamber."

If Esther noticed the impropriety of speaking Logan's first name, she didn't draw attention to it. Her face softened. The ease in her eyes brought calm to a stressful situation. "Don't worry. Everything will sort itself out. Men hurt themselves all the time and your father's a tough soul."

"Yes, he is," Cecily said.

"I'll address your request personally and have Alfred bring the necessities to Mr. Carleton's room."

"Thank you, Esther."

Cecily left the kitchen and retraced her steps to the upper floor. She found her mother in the drawing room and told her the news. She didn't accompany her mother to her parents' bedchamber. It wouldn't be appropriate. Instead, Cecily waited in the drawing room for Logan's re-appearance.

CHAPTER TWENTY-TWO

*L*ogan stood inside the master's bedchamber, waiting for the butler to arrive. He studied the chamber. The luxury made him uncomfortable. He knew Cecily's family was well-to-do, but he'd never seen such extravagance. No gentleman took a farmer's son, even one that came with veterinary credentials, inside a house of privilege.

He shifted his focus to the patient, but one couldn't avoid glancing at rich dark furnishings, a four-poster bed and royal blue bedding. The coverlet matched the carpet and draperies. A rich contrast to yellow wall coverings and gold-framed paintings.

These trappings of societal wealth made him uncomfortable. Not because he didn't own paintings and furniture, more so because he couldn't give such luxury to Cecily, nor could he offer her the lifestyle she was accustomed to.

Damn it.

Mrs. Carleton led the servants inside the bedchamber. "What happened?" she asked indifferently.

The question irritated John. "A horse bite," he said, scowling at his wife, "but don't worry, Lillian. It's not serious. I have not lost a finger."

"Thank goodness for that. You should be more careful. This close to Christmas…how will you assist with the tree?"

"The blasted tree," John said. "I wish Prince Albert had never brought the tradition to England."

Lillian placed her hands on her hips, asserting her position. "This country we find ourselves living in isn't England. Must I remind you, it's our family tradition now, too."

"Still, a fine way to express your care, by reminding me of household responsibility when my hand needs mending."

"Ahem," Alfred interjected, placing the bowl on the commode. "I have the requested items."

"I've brought boiled water. Shall I pour it in the basin, sir?" Esther asked.

Logan ignored the family issues, saying, "Yes, but only half-full."

The housekeeper poured steaming water into the basin. When the water cooled to a manageable temperature, he reached inside his bag and pulled out a bar of veterinary soap.

"You're not tending my hand if you're using animal products," John said with a grimace.

Logan disregarded the sour look. "More often than not animal products relate to human medicine," he said, choosing to educate rather than lecture while cleaning his hands. He glanced at the housekeeper. "A cloth, please." Esther passed him the cloth. Logan dried his hands then passed the cloth back to the housekeeper. "If you will, please throw out the water and return with the basin."

Esther grabbed the basin and left the bedchamber.

"Now, let's take a look at your hand."

Standing near him, John held out his hand. The poor man was in pain if his quivering fingers were any indication. Logan unwound the bandage carefully, not wanting to cause further discomfort. A nasty injury came into sight: teeth marks, bruised skin, and swelling. Mrs. Carleton left the room. It was probably for the best.

"Lady Luck gave you a nasty impression of her teeth. Do you still want to save her?"

John shrugged. "Yes."

"Some colorful bruising as well," Logan said. "Doesn't look like the horse has brought you much luck."

"Not yet." John winced, giving him a look. "It's not her fault. She's ill, after all. Despite the marks, I don't want to put her down."

Logan thought about that comment, still mulling over how he might save the horse.

"I'm surprised you feel that way," Logan said, examining the palm of his hand. "Some men would have grabbed their gun after a horse bite." He released his hold. "You know, the horse is no more than a farm animal, and it could have taken off your fingers. It could bite you a second time if you're not careful."

"I don't need a lecture. Get on with the care."

Logan placed the bandage on the commode. "You never said what circumstances led to the injury. Were you alone in the stable or was Samuel with you?"

"A man needs to get his rest. Neither of us can address the horse's needs all day and all night."

"You were alone."

"Yes, I suppose I was."

Esther returned with the basin and unobtrusively placed it on the commode.

"I'm willing to take over the care of Lady Luck. If you agree to that arrangement, I'd recommend staying away from the stable until your hand has healed or the situation calms down."

"No one tells me what to do in my own house, even a potential son-in-law." His voice rose with warning, but the comment encouraged Logan to smile.

Esther's eyes widened. Alfred presented a curious expression.

"I see you value control, but for your own good, for your health, you should consider resting your hand. It's difficult to manage life without one."

John gave a nervous chuckle. "I don't respond well to threats."

"That wasn't a threat." Logan stared at John then, his eyes rising while asserting his authority. Men like Mr. Carleton understood strength. "Just presenting the facts for your consideration."

John sighed, expressing his frustration. "Look, Logan, you mean well, but I can't leave the care of my animals in the hands of others. How will I know what's happening?"

"I applaud your responsible nature, I really do, but you have to better trust your staff."

"You sound like Lillian."

"If you had more faith in their abilities, you'd have more free time, time to share with your wife and daughters."

"They'd like that." By the look on John's face, he didn't believe it. Logan let the conversation drop.

"I'll manage their care for now. I'll report to you. I'm willing to assume the responsibility until you can take the reins again. It's best I stay here until the situation resolves itself. One way or the other." He looked at John in a meaningful way. "I'd like to clean your wound now."

"I've already done that."

"Why are you being difficult?" Logan gave John a firm look. "I'm disinfecting, vaccinating, and dressing the wound again. This is important," he emphasized. "If the horse has rabies, you could be infected. I don't mean to cause discomfort or pain, but this will hurt."

"Best you comply, sir," Alfred said hesitantly.

"Will you be needing me to stay, sir?" Esther asked.

"Yes," Logan and John said at the same time.

Logan carefully washed John's hand. He winced, grimaced, too, but did not cry out for the pain. Logan retrieved a bottle of iodine tonic from his bag. "This will sting as well as stain your skin, but if you've been in contact with the rabies virus, the iodine might kill it."

John nodded. "Go ahead then, kill it. I don't need

complications of madness, especially so close to Christmas. Lillian is mad enough about the tree."

"Maybe you should look more closely at a decorated tree." Logan smirked, shook his head, and came close to smiling. He wasn't sure why he found the comment amusing. He held John's hand over the basin, then poured tonic on the wound. John flinched, muttering something incomprehensible.

"Don't worry about it," Logan said. "I'll take care of the tree. My gift to you and your family."

John studied him momentarily. "That's a generous offer. I'll take you up on it. The lady of the house will appreciate it." His mannerism went to a solemn place. "I want to save the horse." His voice rattled out of him. "I'll do anything. I'll go to church if the minister will have me."

"Pass me a cloth, Esther."

When the fabric was in his hand, Logan carefully dried John's hand. "Christmas Eve would be the perfect time to attend. It would make your daughter happy."

Logan watched iodine droplets drip into the water and disperse. The caramel color was as dark as his thoughts. What could he do? He couldn't sugarcoat the situation. He went to his doctor's bag and retrieved a vial of vaccine.

"I need to vaccinate you. Unfortunately, in your injured hand. It will hurt. You'll hate me."

"It's that bad."

Logan pumped the syringe then drew vaccine inside. Grasping John's hand, he inoculated him, injecting the serum in several places around the wound. After he was done, he bandaged the hand.

John eyed him seriously, concern wrinkling his face. "Will I contract rabies?"

"No, you won't. By vaccinating you, we've interrupted the incubation period. However, we must assume Lady Luck is infected, and seriously talk about what to do if this is true."

John slid into a chair near the vanity, sighing.

"Lady Luck bit you, likely infected you. Samuel made a valid point. She could infect other horses that are just as valuable."

"I need to know I've done everything possible."

Logan nodded. "And that's great, you should care about your animals. I just need to know what your wishes are if Lady Luck's symptoms get worse."

"I'd like you to stay. I can pay you well."

Logan only wanted one thing. His daughter. "I'd need to live here, at least until Christmas Eve."

"I need a Christmas miracle."

"I'll do my best to provide one." Logan placed the syringe, soap, and iodine tonic back inside his bag. He supposed John would never be ready to pull the trigger on his horse. "You and I are not through. Just in case my treatment is not effective, I need to inject you again, but with immune globulin."

"Now you're making me feel like a horse."

Logan filled a second syringe and gave John a shot in the arm. When he'd finished, Logan looked at Alfred. "Ensure John rests while I'm gone."

He nodded.

Logan grabbed his bag and left the room.

CECILY WAS PACING in the drawing room when Logan came down the stairs. She hurried to meet him. "How's Papa?" she asked.

"The horse gave him a good bite, but it could have been much worse."

"What happened, Logan?"

Cecily could tell by the look on his face that the situation was serious. "Will he be all right?"

"It's too soon to know, but I'm sure your father will recover. He has a strong will and a family, in the stable and in this house that he's willing to fight for."

"Logan, you're frightening me."

He grasped her hand and gently squeezed. Pleasant sensations warmed her and offered comfort. "Your father may have contracted an illness when the horse bit him. The good news? I vaccinated him and that should protect him."

"You gave my father a needle? And he let you?"

"Yes. For a human, he was a good patient."

"Mother must have enjoyed watching. She's upset about the tree."

"Don't worry. I'll take care of the tree, but it can't happen today."

Logan released her hand and she missed his touch. "I

understand. Do what you need to do. I know the situation is urgent."

Logan embraced her, kissed her on the cheek. "I'm sorry, I need to leave."

He left her then, exiting through the front door. Her arms felt empty without him near.

CHAPTER TWENTY-THREE

*L*ogan retrieved the thoroughbred from the stable and raced across snowy fields toward his family home.

A majestic horse filled his thoughts while sitting astride an equally spirited, yet healthy horse. A well-chiseled head, a lean body and long legs. An animal bred to run. But as wintry winds bristled against his skin and through his hair, Logan worried about John Carleton and his Lady Luck.

How do I regain her health? He whispered silent prayers, worrying there was absolutely nothing he could do. The horse's health was in God's hands.

Logan obtained personal belongings, clothing, and other necessities. He collected medicine that might make a difference, vaccine and immune globulin, and then raced back to Carleton House.

When Logan entered John's stable, purpose spurred him onward; to save one special horse and the foal she carried. Holding his vet bag, he hoped he hadn't forgotten anything. His thoughts were heavy as he came closer to Lady Luck's stall. He placed the bag on the floor and stepped closer to the enclosure. He peered through the wrought-iron rails, gripping the cold metal with his hands.

"All right, Lady Luck. You and me, just the two of us. We have one hell of a fight ahead, but we can beat this illness. I know we can."

Lady Luck's muscles quivered, revealing her agitation. She neighed loudly, bobbing her head, and did a quick turn around the stall.

"Can you help her?"

A sweet sound, music to his ear in the dark of the night, but her voice came as a surprise. "Cecily, you shouldn't be here."

"I was waiting for you, watching for you to return. You came into the yard on Papa's horse and…I had to see you."

The hazy light did little to stem her appeal, but his focus must be on the horse. "It's not safe and Lady Luck needs my attention."

"You shouldn't be alone. What if something happened to you? What if…?"

Logan stared at Cecily, her inquisitive eyes, her brown hair tucked under the bonnet. Winter winds whistled outside the stable but he didn't notice the drafty air, his attention on the prettiest lady he'd ever seen. She should leave, but he wanted her to stay. "If anything were to happen to you…" To Cecily? His heart would break.

She nodded. "I understand why you'd be concerned, but I'll be careful. You'll be careful. Logan, it's time I helped in the stable. Is there any reason why I shouldn't?"

Logan jumped down from the stall, offering her a slight smile. He could give her a thousand reasons to stay, one important reason to leave. "A sophisticated woman like you, wearing fine clothing, linen and lace, giving a horse a needle or mucking out a stall. I can't see it happening."

Cecily crossed her arms and made a face as if amused by his comment. She leaned toward him, touching his chest. "It's time I learned." She pointed at herself. "Look at me, I'm wearing gear appropriate for the stable, or a barn. And if…"

"If what?"

"Logan, I need to learn the skills of an animal whisperer." She paused. "After all, I'll need further responsibilities once I become your wife."

His wife? Logan grasped her hand and held it close to his heart. Her words caused his smile to widen. He'd welcome her into his life, but he couldn't imagine her whispering to farm animals or wearing clothing of lesser quality. How could he afford such luxuries as linen or lace?

"Why are you looking at me like that?"

Logan returned his attention to the horse. He released her hand. "Cecily, I can't imagine a woman as sweet as you carrying a pitchfork, let alone using it. A farmer's wife cares for farm animals. She helps with sick horses."

Her expression became serious. "Give me one good reason why I can't? We're courting. All that matters to me is being with you. You can teach me the skills I don't already know."

All he wanted was a kiss, but this sweet woman distracted him from more pressing matters. She shouldn't be here. She was muddling his head with visions of sugar plums. "There's a lot I'd like to teach you. I'd have no issue with messy lessons, but your father might. You're a lady."

"He's given his support."

Logan shook his head. Cecily was too close to him. She looked appealing, her lips tempting him, totally kissable. He yearned to hug her, hold her, never let her go. When Lady Luck neighed loudly, his focus shifted to the horse.

Cecily came closer, moving to his side. "What will you do?"

"I'll inoculate her again. A second dose of rabies vaccine. Another dose of immune globulin."

"Good luck with that. Look at her…she's uncomfortable.

Lady Luck might not accept you in the stall, let alone a needle in the neck. Logan, you could get hurt, like…my father."

He saw the way her brows furrowed, expressing her concern for him, but that wouldn't stop him from doing what was necessary. He hugged her to his side, grasping her waist. "Are you worried about me?"

"Of course, I don't want anything to happen to you."

"I'll be careful," Logan promised. "Would you mind getting Samuel? I'll need his help."

"It's the least I can do," Cecily said. She left the stable to do his bidding.

SAMUEL JOINED Logan near the stall. "Do you have a plan? Are we ending this?"

Logan shook his head but didn't anger. "You have no right asking such an impertinent question. Mr. Carleton wants everything possible done to save this horse's life, so that's what we're going to do. Do you have a problem with the plan?"

"I have a problem with an animal suffering."

Logan kicked at the muck beside the stall. "Look, animals get sick, no different than humans, but we don't end a life because someone is suffering."

Samuel snorted. Maybe the horse's illness had strained him. He sighed. "What do you have in mind?"

"We'll bathe the horse with water and try to make it more comfortable, and then, more immune therapy."

"You won't get anywhere near that horse."

"Not with a poor attitude."

"If you're not man enough to do it, I will," Cecily interjected. "Logan, tell me. What do you need?"

Logan was amazed. Cecily stood before the two men with her hands on her hips, determination and fire in her eyes. He didn't want to rob her of her desire to help. "We need water."

"All right, let's go, Samuel."

Samuel seemed completely gobsmacked that a lady had muscle. He didn't say a word while following Cecily toward the well.

When they returned, each of them was carrying a bucket. Cecily struggled under the weight, but smiled while passing the bucket to Logan. Her father would be proud. He opened the stall and went inside. Lady Luck neighed but didn't show signs of attacking. He poured the first and second buckets of water onto her back. Several buckets later, all three of them were exhausted. It was a lot of work carrying water, let alone throwing it over a horse's back.

Cecily was beat, yet she didn't complain. She gave him a thumbs-up and a sweet but tired smile.

"We need to muck out the stall," Logan said with a grimace, not wanting to ask more of her than she could give.

Cecily grabbed a wheelbarrow. Samuel fetched two shovels. Lady Luck tolerated their presence as they removed debris from the stall.

"Are you all right, Cecily?" Logan asked. "You should rest. You've done enough."

"Not until Lady Luck has been fully cared for." She ran a

hand across a brow spotted with perspiration, leaving a trail of dirt. Logan hoped it was dirt marring her pretty face. The harder she worked, the more he fell in love with her.

"Now what?" Cecily asked.

"Straw for her bed."

Samuel left them to get the straw.

Cecily sighed, then reached for a pitchfork. She wavered on her feet while holding it in her hands.

"Take a rest, lass."

He retrieved the pitchfork, and Cecily didn't complain. She leaned against the opposite stall, too tired to do anything more.

Logan and Samuel filled the stall with bedding. The entire time, Lady Luck tolerated the intrusion.

BY THE TIME Logan held the syringe, everyone was exhausted. He grasped the stall door. "Now, don't do anything foolish. Are you ready?"

"I'm ready. Be fast and be careful."

Logan focused on the horse. "Play nice, Lady Luck."

Logan opened the gate and entered the stall. The horse shimmied away, but Samuel kept hold of the rope, keeping it taut. He didn't want to spook the horse. Neither did he want a bite wound. The horse neighed, tossed its head.

"Easy girl," Logan said, stepping closer, clutching the syringe in his hand.

When Lady Luck kicked her hind legs, he retreated a bit. "I'm not trying to hurt you."

"Do you think she understands what you're saying, horse whisperer?" Cecily asked. "Or is she eyeing your needle?"

"Aye, she felt it before. She knows something's up."

Lady Luck made her feelings known when she stomped her right foot and stepped backward a bit, but Logan was undeterred. He stepped forward, grasped a fold of skin, and plunged the needle into her neck. The surprise move frightened her, and she flung her head and rose onto her hind legs. "Damn," Logan said, forced to release the syringe. But somehow, it stayed in her neck.

He only needed to press the plunger.

"Pull the rope taut," Logan yelled.

"I'm trying, but she's fighting me." Samuel wrestled with the line.

Logan sprinted forward, then jumped back, dancing with the horse. He waited for the opportune moment. After a time, Lady Luck's temperament improved, permitting Logan to empty the syringe.

He left the stall and Samuel shut the gate. "Well hell, how did you manage that? I've never seen a horse go so docile."

"He's a horse whisperer, Samuel," Cecily said with a giggle.

"That horse," Logan said, breathing hard, "is not lucky."

"What do we do now?" Cecily asked.

"We wait. If she receives this second dose well, we'll give her another in two days, and another two days after that."

"That will bring us close to Christmas Eve."

Logan nodded. "Hopefully, I'll give your family something positive to celebrate."

All they needed was a little lady luck.

CHAPTER TWENTY-FIVE

Cecily was in the dining room, having breakfast with her family when Alfred came into the room. "Mr. Campbell is here to see you, sir."

"Let him in," John said.

"Into the dining room?"

"Yes, Alfred."

Abigail nudged Cecily's foot under the table. This was an exciting development. She tried to keep a straight face, but joy filled her heart that Logan wove a path into her life and their private dining room. She was happy to see him: his handsome face, his denim work clothes. She glanced at his hips, understanding the impropriety of the look. She smiled.

"Good morning, Logan," Mr. Carleton said, placing his fork on the table.

"Good morning, John," Logan replied.

"Do you have news for me?"

"Yes, I sure do."

"I hope it's good." John directed him to a nearby chair. "Why don't you take a seat. Alfred, give Logan some tea." Father returned his attention to Logan. "Have you broken your morning fast?"

"No time for food."

"You remind me of someone else at this table." Cecily gave her father a meaningful look.

John laughed. "Footman, feed this man."

"As you wish, sir." Alfred poured tea into a cup. Albert spooned eggs, bacon, and beans onto Logan's plate.

"Would you like milk with your tea, Mr. Campbell?"

"No, thank you. I prefer mine black."

John drummed his fingers on the table, his facial expression becoming more severe and thoughtful. "Tell me about Lady Luck."

"I managed to give her a second vaccination yesterday. She was testy, but I succeeded."

"Great news. How's she faring today?"

Logan poked at the eggs on his plate. "The vaccine combined with the immune therapy might be working. She's calmer, less agitated. The fever has fallen. The spasms have eased. She's sleeping while standing upright."

John sighed. "So still some depression. I'm grateful for more hopeful news. I was worried about that horse."

"Samuel and I are doing everything we can. How's your hand?"

"Sore as hell. Still quite swollen. I feel tired."

"I'll take a look at it before I leave as I need to give you another dose anyway."

"Is that necessary?"

"Unfortunately, yes."

"John, I'd like to keep the promise I made and help your family with getting the tree. I can spare the time now."

Even before John could respond, Abigail clapped her hands.

"It appears someone is happy with this news," John said.

"I know you're hurt, Papa, but I'm excited Christmas is near. I know Logan will make it extra special."

John raised his eyes. "A tree makes the season special?"

"Abigail likes the small candles on the branches, especially when they're lit," Cecily said. "Come on, Papa, you must agree, it's pretty."

"It's a fire hazard and extra work."

"There's always work during the Christmas season. I know you enjoy Christmas pudding."

"That I do," John said, rubbing his belly. "When will the search begin?"

"After breakfast," Logan replied. "Thank you, John, for having me at your table."

CHAPTER TWENTY-SIX

ogan was preparing to leave Carleton House when an idea came to him. He returned to the dining room and faced the family. "I offered to get your tree, but for the Campbells, tree-gathering is a family tradition. We always go into the forest together to find our tree. It doesn't feel right getting the tree without you. Why don't you come with me?"

John grunted, making a face. "While I have participated in the selection process, the servants always find and decorate the tree. We enjoy the final look."

"What fun is that?" Logan asked.

"It's the way things are done, the way they have always been done."

"This is new land, a chance to build new traditions."

"I want to go," Abigail said, rising from her chair. "Can we?"

Father's eyebrows rose. He remained on his chair. "I

suppose you want to experience new traditions as well, Cecily."

"It could be fun." Cecily smirked, eyeing her father. She could tell Logan wanted her to accompany him. It was a beautiful day. This was a perfect opportunity to spend more time together, especially since they had a reprieve in horse care.

"Even if I were open to the idea, look at me, look at this useless hand."

"I bet you don't get out much. You probably haven't had a chance to prepare for the Christmas season. Come on, John. Try something new. Do something special for your family."

"Something special?"

"I can drive. I can chop down the tree. Cecily and I are in the choir; we can lead you in a rousing rendition of carols."

"I can't sing," Mrs. Campbell said, having been silent up until this point.

"Logan and I need to practice for Christmas Eve. You can listen to us again."

"It caused some emotion in me the first time. There's been enough emotion lately," John said.

Cecily said, "Don't worry, Papa, there's other songs to sing, happier songs."

"What a fabulous idea," Abigail said. "Please, Papa. Can we do it?"

"All right," John said, smiling. "Who am I to hinder the Christmas tree hunt."

ONCE EVERYONE HAD BROKEN their fast, Logan gave Cecily's father a second dose of vaccine and more immune globulin. Then, the entire Carleton family dressed in warm winter clothing: coats, scarves, hats, and gloves. They bundled into the Campbell sleigh and set off on a journey across snow-laden fields to find the perfect tree. Cecily knew this journey would make her father happy. Logan's offer had given him the perfect opportunity to approve the tree, even though unbeknownst to him, the decision had already been made.

What had inspired his change of heart?

Logan's draft horse soon set off, trotting toward the Campbell land. Its large hooves kicked up snow, but that wasn't what made the trip special. Logan had added bells to the horse's halter. Cecily listened to the jingling sound while studying her family. She couldn't recall the last time they had taken a ride together in the same conveyance. She had Logan to thank for this.

She glanced at him. He seemed comfortable in the presence of her family. Maybe his pleasant attitude had something to do with the horse's improved health. His assistance not only made changes in an animal's life, but also her family's. Maybe he was a human whisperer, too.

Holding the reins, Logan gave her a happy, relaxed look. "Do you like the jingle?"

"Very much. It's a pleasant sound."

"A fine day for a ride," Logan said.

John seemed more interested in the horse than the passing trees. "She's a fine workhorse. Strong. How many hands high?"

"Sixteen. Her name's Molly. She gets the work done."

"Plowing the fields and such?"

"Yes."

"The weather seems to have cooperated," Cecily said, giving Logan a wink. "One never knows when the wind will blow."

"Another snow storm?" Abigail interjected. "Don't jinx us so close to Christmas."

Logan glanced at Cecily, eyeing her family. "Tell me about your Christmas traditions. What do you enjoy the most?"

John pondered the question. "I'm in the stable half the time. The Christmas meal makes me a happy man: pork roast, candied yams, I always look forward to the Christmas pudding."

Logan clicked his tongue, encouraging the horse to run. "Ah…mixed fruit, with the addition of some type of spirit?"

"Bourbon," Cecily said. "It adds a nice spice."

Mother had bound herself in a long winter fur with a muff surrounding her hands. Her fingers tapped in time to the jingling bells. "I enjoy having my family around the table. Candlelight. Wine. It's the one time of year we're close."

Abigail's facial expression turned wistful. "I love the color, the decorations and the light. I can't wait to put tinsel and candles on the tree."

"My sister, Isla, has been making garlands of cranberries and popcorn," Logan said. "My mother likes it. Keeps her small hands busy."

"Do you want to sing, Logan?" Cecily asked.

"I'd like that."

"O Holy Night on three…one, two, three."

"O holy night…the stars are brightly shining—" Their voices blended perfectly together. No one interrupted them as they sang. The sleigh slid smoothly through the snow and Molly's trot, trot, trotting rhythm pounded against the frozen earth like the beat of the drum. Cecily almost forgot her family was in the sleigh.

When they reached the second verse, Logan gestured with his hand, "Won't you join us?"

"A thrill of hope, the weary world rejoices—"

Father didn't know the words, or if he did, he'd forgotten them. Lillian sang, but off-key. Abigail sang, but a little too loudly. Cecily didn't think she'd ever shared a moment like this with her family. Her heart filled with joy. She saddened when the song ended. Her family's joy was more potent than the singing.

Logan pulled on the reins, urging the horse and the sleigh to a stop. "I passed by this tree earlier and thought it would be perfect for your drawing room. What do think, John?"

"Can we get it, Papa?" Abigail asked hopefully.

"It's a nice tree, but I don't think so," John said. "It's not on our land."

Cecily dared to be honest. "Papa, we actually saw the tree on stir-it-up Sunday. Abigail fell in love with it." Though to be honest, her sister was more in love with Ian.

"Still, it's not on our land."

"John, it would be my pleasure to give you this tree. My gift."

"Are you sure?"

"Yes."

"What do you think, Lillian?" John asked. "Does the tree please you as much as our daughter?"

"It's perfect."

Logan shifted the brake into place and left the sleigh. He quickly felled the tree and hooked it to the back of the sleigh.

When they were underway again, John said, "This has been a pleasant experience. What do you think, girls, should we make it a yearly tradition?"

Abigail clapped.

"It's a great idea," Cecily said, "but only if Logan drives the sleigh."

"I'll be here," Logan said, eyeing Cecily. "With bells on."

CHAPTER TWENTY-SEVEN

Three days prior to Christmas Eve, Cecily and Abigail were in the drawing room, placing decorations on the tree. Carleton House overflowed with festive trimmings. Gold ribbons, silver tinsel, and branches giving off the scent of balsam fir, but decorations hadn't brought comfort and joy. Something more meaningful stirred Cecily's emotions.

Holding a crystal ornament in her hands, she pondered her parents. When was the last time she'd seen them like this? In companionable silence? Father reading the morning paper. Mother sipping tea.

Suddenly, her musings were interrupted by someone knocking at the door. Her attention shifted to the entranceway. When Alfred escorted Logan into the drawing room, her heart thumped with joy.

"She's better," he said.

"Who?" John asked, lowering his newspaper. Cecily was

certain her father knew what Logan suggested, but he waited for the good news all the same.

"Lady Luck! Her health has rallied for the better. Her fever is down, the spasms have stopped. Samuel managed to get a turnip into her this morning."

"This is good news," John said, rising from his chair. He came forward and shook Logan's hand. "I am in your debt, sir."

"Nah," Logan replied, swiping the air with his fingers. "You don't owe me anything. I'm so happy I could celebrate. Cecily, should we sing? Abigail, play us a tune on the piano."

Abigail laughed. "Not right now. Not until we've finished decorating the tree."

"I'll have to take on other pursuits then."

A twinkle in Logan's eye forewarned Cecily that he had an objective in mind. He moved toward her with a determined look. She didn't know whether she should be excited or afraid. But when he reached for her and grasped her around the waist, she gasped. "Logan…" He lifted her into the air, embracing her in an affectionate hug.

She giggled, kicking her feet. "Put me down. My parents are here, they're watching, and Abigail and I are decorating the tree."

He whistled. "Can't believe it's the same tree. You ladies have done wonderful work." He nestled near her ear. "It's not as gorgeous as you," Logan said, whispering.

Cecily touched his nose, smiling, her cheeks a hue of pink. "You're a rascal. There's more to do, but since you're here and Lady Luck's health has improved, why don't you help?

We were just placing tinsel and crystal ornaments. You're taller than us. You can reach the higher branches."

Cecily's father snickered, as if he was enjoying his own moment of humor.

Logan placed her on her feet but kept one hand on her waist. He drew something from his coat pocket. "What's so funny, Papa? Something must be. I haven't heard you laugh like that in a long time."

He stared directly at her. "You're under the mistletoe. You know what that means, you have to kiss your gentleman."

"Right now? In front of you?" Cecily was horrified with the prospect. Sure, she wanted to kiss Logan, but not in front of her parents. It was terribly improper.

"That's the way it's usually done," her mother said, giggling. "You know the rules, Cecily. Don't keep Logan waiting."

"In front of my family? I couldn't possibly."

"John, might I have permission to kiss your daughter?"

Father gazed at her mother. "What do you think, Lillian? Is it appropriate? They're not even engaged."

Her mother smiled, stifling a laugh. "What's going on here?" Cecily asked.

Father grasped her mother's hand. "You have our blessing. To kiss beneath the mistletoe."

"Come here, lass," Logan said, holding mistletoe in his hand. He placed the magic above her head and grasped her left hand.

"It doesn't work this way," Cecily said, trying to understand what was happening. "You can't bring mistletoe into the house and place it above my head. The mistletoe kiss must be a surprise encounter."

But then Cecily saw something sparkling in the greenery. Logan knelt to his knees, still holding her hand. "Cecily Carleton, will you marry me? I'm no more than a farmer's son. I can't give you everything you deserve, but I promise to love you for the rest of my life."

Cecily studied the seriousness on Logan's face. She glanced at her parents and saw her father nod. No one made a sound while waiting for her to say something.

"Cecily…"

"Yes, Logan, horse whisperer, I'll marry you."

Logan unfastened the ring from the red ribbon. Cecily extended her left hand, her fingers quivering as he placed a gorgeous diamond solitaire on her finger. How could he afford such a gem? Then under the mistletoe, Logan gave her a chaste kiss, and though the embrace was brief, the caress fired warmth in her heart.

"Congratulations," Father said, rising from his chair a second time.

"We're happy for you." Mother rose from her chair as well.

"Much love, always," Abigail hastened to add. "I can't wait for Christmas, though it's not entirely fair, Cecily has received her heart's desire early."

"What's that?" Logan asked.

"A gentleman for Christmas."

CHAPTER TWENTY-EIGHT

People wandered into the church sanctuary, thirsty for the word. Christmas Eve was the most important service of the year. The parishioners were eager to hear the minister's Christmas message, to hear special songs from the choir and celebrate the meaning of it all while gathering as a community.

Though her nerves were as fragile as Mary's spirits must have been on one holy night, Cecily only had one objective in mind for this evening, to get through the performance without making a mistake. Could they do it?

She stamped the worry down while waiting to enter the sanctuary. Standing among the choir members in the choral room, she listened to the clatter echoing from the sanctuary. The constant buzz made her curious to know how many people had chosen to attend the service. She left Logan's side and crept toward the archway, which led into the sanctuary.

She peered beyond the doorway, surprised to see that most

pews were full. Not one vacant seat. The larger the audience, the more people to critique their performance. This concern would only add to Logan's discomfort. She glanced at him, certain terror had struck him speechless. Would he be able to sing? She hoped he'd find the courage to breathe, to recognize his voice and enjoy his first duet in front of the congregation.

Though returning her sightline to the pews, she saw a few members in attendance would add joy to the occasion. Hopefully… His family sat near the front. Her family sat near the back, even her father who rarely came to this spiritual place.

Change was in the air and Cecily couldn't be happier. She stepped back inside the choir room.

"Are you ready?" Cecily asked, giving Logan a supportive look.

He shrugged. His hands were quivering. "I've never been so nervous. I don't know what's wrong with me. It's far easier caring for animals. What if I embarrass myself? What if I forget the words? What if I disappoint you?"

Cecily tried to offer her support. "It's okay, Logan. No one will throw rotten food if you make a mistake."

"I didn't imagine that could happen." He looked more worried now than ever.

Cecily couldn't help herself, she giggled. She squeezed his arm. "Hey, I'll be right beside you, supporting you. We can read off the paper if that makes you more comfortable."

He shook his head. "No, I'll not read words from a paper. We'll make more of an impression if we don't have props in our hands. What if I lose my place? The paper might only get in our way."

"Just the two of us, then? Are you certain?"

Logan nodded. "With you beside me… Aye, Cecily. I'm ready."

Ruth rushed into the choral room. "Are we ready?" she asked. Cecily didn't know why Ruth whispered. The noise beyond the choir had risen to a crescendo.

"We're ready." Logan replied.

"Let's go then."

Cecily took one final look at Logan and offered him a supportive look, then one by one, the choir filed into the sanctuary and took their seats. This movement signaled to those in attendance that the service was about to begin.

ALTHOUGH THE MINISTER delivered the Christmas message, Cecily hardly heard a word. A star in the night sky burning bright, guiding wise men toward hope. Snippets of the Christmas story, Mary and Joseph, and the journey they'd made on an evening such as this. Faith for the masses, peace for the people, hope, and *love*. Love—Cecily glanced at Logan at the mention of the word, grateful for the affection she'd found with the gentleman sitting beside her. Her Christmas gift, gifts to cherish, gifts of love, were difficult to find.

And then the moment arrived. They rose from their chairs, moved toward the congregation, and settled into song.

"O holy night…"

Though an entire community stared at them, Cecily didn't concern herself with the perusal. Just like they'd sung the hymn in front of her parents, they focused on each other. She held Logan's hand the entire time, feeling his fingers quivering in her grasp. She squeezed his hand, focusing only on the carol and the man she sang it with, letting Logan know simply from a handhold that he wasn't alone. She stood right beside him.

Though Cecily's stance didn't change anything. His fingers quivered, even during the middle verses, though his voice sang out sweetly. She listened to the beauty of it. His smooth intonation, the sound as mellow as a lune calling to a mate at sunset.

When they delivered the last note, leaving their audience in suspended excitement, they stared at each other for a few moments. Wonder in his eyes. Love in his expression. The silence stretched in the sanctuary… But when they broke apart, preparing to return to their seats, the congregation applauded their performance.

Logan smiled, taking a breath of air. That's the moment her heart filled with complete and utter joy. Cecily knew she'd go anywhere with this man. To a stable in Bethlehem, even a barn in the back woods of Essex. Life wouldn't be complete without him, and she'd already proven she could carry a shovel.

CHAPTER TWENTY-NINE

On Christmas day, the Carleton family engaged in conversation around the dinner table in the same way they had every other Christmas season; even so, something had changed. An extra section was added to the table, making room for additional guests. Logan joined them. His parents and his siblings, too.

Joy and laughter filled the dining room and Father's favorite foods: roasted pork, minced pies, dates and figs and sweet breads were plentiful.

Little Isla couldn't be still and raced around the table with an older brother. It amused Cecily to no end watching the children have fun. Isla carried a new doll. Her brother held a small metal soldier. Cecily glanced at her father, listening to his laughter while wondering why he'd chosen to invite the Campbells into their home, let alone bestow on them goodwill and gifts.

"You see that, Cecily," father said, gesturing toward her

and Logan, "this time next year, your mother and I would like to have a grandchild running around the table."

"Sounds wonderful." Alfred sighed, trying to place a platter of Christmas pudding on the table.

Cecily's eyebrows rose. "It's more likely a foal will be frolicking in the pasture."

The mention of the foal had her father staring at Logan as if her fiancé was a saint. Lady Luck's health continued to improve, which gave her father an even greater reason to celebrate.

"Have you set the date yet?" her grandmother asked.

Logan grasped Cecily's hand. "You can expect a spring wedding. We won't start construction on the house until the ground thaws."

Father said, "Do you have designs yet? Where will you build?"

Wintry winds had blown away some of their imaginary concept at a patch of land near the lake. It was a fine place to build a home. Smack dab in the center of Campbell and Carleton land.

"We haven't decided on the location," Logan said, glancing at her.

"You're welcome to build on Carleton land."

Mr. Campbell Senior cleared his throat. "Campbell land is equally suitable."

"A place in the middle of both properties might be best." Cecily took a sip of her wine. "In this way, we'll be close to both of our families and not hurt anyone's feelings by choosing either family."

Logan rose from his chair, holding his wine goblet. "I agree wholeheartedly. A toast to the future. May all your days be merry."

Cecily stood, too. "And all your evenings bright. Merry Christmas, everyone."

Thank you for reading *A Gentleman for Christmas*.
If you enjoyed Logan and Cecily's love story, your honest opinion of their romance matters to this author. Please review this book on your favorite book site, review site, blog, or your own social media properties, and share your opinion with other readers.

A sincere *thank you* for taking the time to write a review!

NOTES

201

CHAPTER 7

1. *All Things Bright and Beautiful*, Cecil Frances Alexander, 1848.

AUTHOR'S NOTE

The premise of this story began with my mom. As an employee and manager of Royal Doulton for nearly thirty years, she has an exquisite collection of figurines. When I was searching for ideas for this novel, there was no better place to look than her home. One figurine from the Carol Singers collection inspired me: "*God Rest Ye, Merry Gentlemen.*" This couple also inspired the novel's title: *A Gentleman for Christmas.*

In the early 1900s, a woman managed her house and family. Cecily wasn't likely to make Christmas pudding with her grandmother, but given that my mother remembers doing so, this was important for me to include. A woman was also likely involved in church life, which encouraged me to have Cecily in the choir, of which I have some experience, having sung in a choir as well.

Finding a husband would be a primary effort, and class

and racial divisions were prevalent in the early 1900s as they are now.

It was fascinating researching equine illness as it gave me a better understanding of rabies. After four years of research, Louis Pasteur developed a vaccine in 1885. It rapidly became used around the world and is still used today as an effective treatment. The fascinating part about the vaccine is that it not only protects people and animals from the illness prior to a bite, but also protects after the bite, as the inoculation interrupts the incubation period, which is around two weeks. But once symptoms are prevalent, rabies is almost always fatal.

I've taken a bit of leniency in my Christmas story, to save Lady Luck, to give John Carleton a Christmas miracle, and Cecily...*A Gentleman for Christmas*.

I hope you enjoyed this insight into my Christmas story.

CONTACT SHELLEY KASSIAN

If you would like to learn more about Shelley or her novels, visit her website at shelleykassian.com. Here you can read excerpts from her books, linked reviews, blog posts, as well as discovering her professional affiliations and accreditation.

Shelley enjoys hearing from her readers. If you'd like to contact the author, please send her a message at: shelleykassian@gmail.com.

FOLLOW SHELLEY ON SOCIAL MEDIA

amazon.com/author/shelleykassian

goodreads.com/shelleykassian

facebook.com/ShelleyKassian

instagram.com/shelleykassian

twitter.com/@shelleykassian

linkedin.com/in/shelleykassian

pinterest.com/shelleykassian

ABOUT SHELLEY KASSIAN

Bestselling author Shelley Kassian has been writing timeless love stories filled with romance or dark fantasy (romantasy) for more than twenty years, novels that include her recent true love story, *A Mountain Leads Home*. A history enthusiast, she's traveled far and wide to explore secret gardens and medieval castles, having an avid interest in the Tudor period. Her prose has been described as "near rhapsodic," "pitch perfect," and "stylishly straightforward, rarely relying on complex turns of phrase." Reviewers have said her narrative conveys "imaginative fantasy," "fascinating characters," and "refreshing romance."

Shelley's taken creative writing courses, holds board positions within professional associations, and retains a Professional Editing Certificate. Drawing on her expertise, she has mentored novice writers, but her passion comes alive while scribing her stories into novel-length fiction. Shelley shares her life with her husband, adores her adult children and two grand pups, and when not relaxing at her seaside cottage, lives in Calgary, Alberta, Canada.

www.ingramcontent.com/pod-product-compliance
Lightning Source LLC
Chambersburg PA
CBHW021327190726
48288CB00003B/992